Body Swap

Book 3

I Want My Body Back!!!

Katrina Kahler

Table of Contents

The Skate Park

Skate Park. 8pm. Come alone.

That's what the text from Tom said. The first text I had received from him in days. At first, I just stared at my phone in shock. Was it broken? Was this some kind of fluke? I texted him back after running around my bedroom a few times in excitement.

R U sure?

I waited, kneeling on my bed and clutching the phone in front of me, staring at the screen. Slow minutes passed. It could have been hours. It *might* have been hours. I refused to take my eyes from the screen.

BUZZ BUZZ.

"Agh!" I dropped the phone on my bed when the next text came through. It bounced harmlessly off my pillow. I scrambled to pick it back up and opened the message. One word flashed on the screen in front of me:

Yeah.

I let out a loud laugh, waving the phone in the air in triumph. Bursting out of my room, I rushed downstairs, taking the steps two at a time, the wind rushing past my face as I sped to the bottom. I burst into the living room, the door swinging open and banging against the wall. Dad turned from the sofa, his face a deep frown.

"Jack, you can't just run around the house-"

I didn't let him finish.

"It's happening!" I grinned at him, shaking the phone in his direction.

"What's happening?" he asked.

I smiled wider. "I'm getting my best friend back!"

OK, so maybe I was a *little* over-excited. I realized this when I arrived at the skate park and checked my phone. It was 7:30pm. I was early. *Really* early. To make things worse, the sky had turned a blotchy dark gray above me and the first pitter-patter of drops fell onto my head. It was going to rain. Typical.

By 7:45pm, I was glad that my dad's selection of coats were all practical and waterproof (even if they did look *ridiculous*). I had picked a black one that had a weird red fish on the front. It was the least offensive of all of them. I now did the zip right up to my chin and pulled the hood over my head as the sky opened and released as much rain as it could. It was like standing under a waterfall. I blinked raindrops off my eyelashes, but all I could see were streams of horizontal rain. Everyone in the skate park ran for shelter. I was left alone.

By 8:05pm, I felt certain that I was being set up and that this was an elaborate ploy by ninjas to assassinate me (I don't overreact! What are you talking about?). Every movement catching my eye seemed more evidence of something dark and dangerous prowling the skate park, waiting to catch me. As I stood shivering in the entrance to the park, I seriously considered going back home.

"Why are you standing in the rain?"

I jumped a mile into the sky when Tom appeared behind me. "Don't *do* that!" I shouted over the rattle of the rain on the ground around us. "You scared the life out of me!"

When I had recovered my senses, Tom beckoned me over to a nearby bike shed where we sheltered from the rain.

"Jack?" he finally said after a pause.

"The one and only," I grinned back at him. He had been confused ever since the school fair last week, when he had found out about the *incident*. I had tried explaining it to him, over and over: my dad and I had been struck by lightning and swapped bodies. It wasn't *that* hard to understand, right? Still, it had taken him a while to... recover from what he had learned. I mean, if anyone had looked at this bike shed, they would have seen Tom, a 12-year-old boy

4

wearing a t-shirt with our favorite band's logo on it, and Mr. David Stevenson – teacher in his late thirties, in an old waterproof coat. An old waterproof coat that I was now learning had *holes* in it. Great.

"So you're Jack," he said again.

"Still yes. And my dad is me. Not Jack. I am Jack." I frowned. I was beginning to confuse myself.

"No," Tom said, leaning against an abandoned BMX. "This is crazy."

"Believe me, I know," I nodded. To Tom, I probably looked like a crazy old man who had lost his mind. But my dad had confirmed my story. Didn't that count for something?

"Prove it," Tom said. "Prove that I'm not going crazy right now."

"What about all the weird things I have been doing at school?" I asked. "I've been *enjoying* Math, haven't I? Would I ever do that?"

Tom nodded. "That's true, but maybe you just... maybe you just caught a virus or something that made you *like* Math!"

I shivered. What a horrible thought: *liking* Math.

"Tell me something only Jack and I would know!" he said.

A slow grin spread across my face. This was going to be easy. The skate park was where Tom and I had spent a *lot* of our childhood. If there was anywhere I could prove myself, it was here. I stuck out a finger into the rain and pointed at some nearby stairs. "That is where I nearly broke my leg trying to impress Holly by standing on the stair rail. When my dad asked what had happened, you told him I hurt it helping a cat out of a tree."

The corner of Tom's mouth twitched as he remembered the story. "Yeah, I guess."

I kept going, pointing at a half pipe on the other side of the park. "That was where we almost had a fight once

5

because we thought a hot girl liked both of us, until it turned out she was just trying to get us to give her money for ice cream. Her name was..." I blinked. What *was* her name? I frowned.

"Tabby, short for Tabatha," Tom grinned openly now. "I would have won that fight."

"If you say so," I grinned back.

Tom stared out into the park. "This is *so* weird. I mean, you're an *adult*."

"I know, right?"

"You tried to drive yet?"

"I did. Almost got arrested."

"Wow."

"I know."

Even though it was raining, I felt like the sun was shining and this was a beautiful day. I hadn't been able to speak to anyone like this (apart from my *dad*) for weeks, and talking to an adult was like talking to a boring brick wall sometimes.

I sighed. "You have no idea how great it is to talk to someone about this. Things are going to be so much *easier* now."

Tom turned to me and frowned. "How long have you been in your dad's body?"

"Since before the school dance," I told him.

"Woah," Tom said. "So everything that has happened since then... Playing the drums in band, that whole thing with Jasmine, the weird way that you actually did school work and did it so well that you actually got everything right..."

"Yep," I nodded. "All Dad in my body."

Tom looked like his whole world had been thrown into a washing machine, spun around a hundred times and then left hanging upside down to dry. "Huh," he said. "That answers a *lot* of questions."

"I know, right?" I agreed.

6

Tom's eyes narrowed. "Wait..." he took a step forward and poked me in the chest. "Who has been *dating my mom then?!?*"

Uh oh.

I backed away into the rain. "Well, listen, it's not that simple... I mean we went to the movies once, but..."

"YOU WENT TO THE MOVIES WITH MY MOM?" Tom shouted.

It wasn't going as planned. I backed away a bit more and glanced at my wrist. "Oh, look at the time, I've got to get back home. Curfew and stuff."

Tom stalked after me. "You aren't wearing a watch, Jack! Get back here!"

"Gottagobye!" I said quickly, turning and running to the entrance of the skate park.

I heard Tom shouting my name, demanding I return, and I couldn't help but smile. It was great to have my best friend back.

Time for a Holiday

I was *soaked* when I got back, but I was still grinning. Tom would get over it, I was sure. He was talking to me now and that was all that mattered. Triumphantly, I entered the living room. My dad was still sitting where I had left him, staring at the TV (that was off) with a strange expression that I had never seen on his (well... my) face before. It looked like he was lost in a deep thought, and that thought wasn't a happy one. I decided to snap him out of it by throwing the coat over his head.

"I'm baaack!" I said cheerfully as he fought to get the soaking wet coat off himself.

When he finally yanked it away, his hair wet and stuck to his head, he scowled at me and threw it back. "Hang that up, Jack," he scolded me. "You're making the sofa wet!"

For once, it didn't suck to be scolded by Dad. I just smiled and picked up the coat and hung it on the hook in the hallway.

"Did you have fun while I was out?" I joked. "Life must be *boring* for you when I'm not around."

Dad rolled his eyes. "How do I cope without you?" He stood up and punched me playfully on the shoulder. "Listen, Jack," he said, his tone serious. "I've been thinking..." he paused, avoiding my gaze.

What was up with him? He looked like he was about to reveal the biggest secret of his life. I secretly hoped that I was an alien from another planet and had awesome super powers, but instead he just seemed to snap out of it and said, "How about we go on a holiday?"

I was stunned for a second. Dad didn't *do* holidays. Unless you counted a short road trip to the nearest museum. He always likes to say that *learning is fun*, but it isn't. It really, really isn't.

"You don't want to go to the Paper Museum again, do you?" I groaned. "Paper is *not as interesting as you say it is.*"

Dad laughed. "No, no, not there. Although – just because you *don't listen* doesn't mean it *isn't interesting.*" It was an old argument that Dad and I had often. It went a bit like this:

Me: It's boring!
Dad: You just need to listen and take it all in.
Me: If it wasn't boring maybe I would listen more!
Dad: But you don't listen enough.
Me: Because it's boring!
Dad: Because you don't listen!
Etc. etc.

The argument usually goes on for a while until we both give up and go for ice cream.

"Anyway," Dad said, pulling a piece of paper from his pocket. "Remember this?" As he handed it to me, I realized it wasn't a piece of paper, but a photo. It was old and crinkled, probably from years of being stuffed in a drawer.

"Wow," I joked. "Super retro."

The photo was a picture of me and him. I must have been about two years old, and I was sitting on his shoulders. We were both in t-shirts and shorts, and it was a bright sunny day. Behind us was a wooden cabin of some sort and beyond that, I could just make out what looked like a lake. On our faces were the biggest, happiest grins. We looked like we had just won the lottery.

I was surprised. I couldn't remember the last time I had seen Dad grin like that. He almost looked like a completely different person.

"Where was this taken?" I frowned. "I don't

remember this at all."

"That's our cabin. We got it when we lived in Minnesota. Haven't been there since you were... oh... two and a half? It's been quite a few years."

"We have a *cabin*?" I said, surprised. "This is awesome, why didn't you tell me?"

Dad shrugged. "We haven't had the time to go back since. I didn't want you to be disappointed. But with Dr. Turner and his forced holiday time, I thought maybe we could check it out again. See how the old cabin has handled the years without us."

Dr. Turner was the psychiatrist we were sent to by *another* doctor whom we had tried to get to help us out with the whole body swap incident. He had decided (without listening to me) that I had clearly gone crazy, and had given us two weeks to sort it out or he would force us to take a break from work.

Two weeks had gone by. Nothing had changed. Dad was now on 'forced vacation,' which wasn't too bad since the summer break was only a couple of weeks away, but he was clearly anxious about being away from his job. In fact, recently he'd been acting weirder than ever. Maybe a break from all of this *would* do both of us some good. I definitely felt like I could use a little time away.

Dad gave me a smile that seemed forced and was almost creepy. It was like he was *desperate* for me to say yes.

"Alright," I smiled in return. "Let's go rock out at the cabin!"

"Great!" Dad looked relieved.

But then he continued, "Oh...and there's one more thing."

I raised an eyebrow. He was acting really strangely and I wasn't sure what to expect. The odd look on his face was making me nervous. I started to worry, thinking that something was definitely wrong. And then he finally spoke.

"We should take Tom and Sarah with us."

Tom's House

The next day, I stood in front of Tom's large house but I was struggling to climb the steps to his front door. If you've ever seen an old haunted house in a scary movie that is kind of what Tom's house looked like.

It wasn't that I didn't want to go on vacation with Tom. No, the thought of going on holiday with Tom was *awesome*. We would have a great time. It was Sarah that would be the issue. *Yes*, I had been pretending to date her for the last few weeks, and yes, it had been *super weird*, but I was pretending to be Dad then. I had been trying not to wreck Dad's life, just as he had been (poorly) trying not to wreck mine. Tom hadn't known it was me then, but now...

"Maybe they aren't home?" I said.

"You have to *press the doorbell* to find out, Jack. That is the point of doorbells," Dad replied. "Plus, look," he pointed at Sarah's car in their driveway, "why would they be here and leave their car?"

"But..." I said.

"Push it," said Dad.

"Fine," I groaned.

A tinkling of musical DING DONGs ran through the house. Dad patted me on the shoulder as if he was congratulating a kindergartener. I growled at him and he smirked back at me.

We waited. The urge to run away grew and grew inside me, and I tried to ignore it. I wondered what would happen if I ran away now, right down the street, and never came back. "I think-" I began, but I was interrupted by the door opening and Tom greeting us with a confused look on his face.

"Jack?" he said to me. "Mr. Stevenson?" he said to my dad.

"Hi, Tom," said Dad.

I grimaced. "Run, Tom," I whispered. "Run for your life."

Tom's eyes widened.

"Ha. Ha." Dad said. "Ignore him, Tom. Is your mom in?"

Tom's eyes narrowed. "Why?" he asked suspiciously.

"No reason, let's go!" I spun on my heels, but Dad hooked an arm around my waist and stopped me from moving.

"Tom?" Sarah's voice came from upstairs. "Who is it?"

Tom rolled his eyes. There was no way he was going to be able to keep us out of the house now. "It's Jack and..."

he looked at me. "David. They wanna talk to us about something."

"Well, let them in!" she shouted. "I'll be downstairs in a second."

Tom shook his head and sighed. "Come in, I guess."

Dad walked in in front of me, and Tom pointed him towards the living room. As I was about to enter, he spun around and stood in my way. "No funny stuff," he said. "That's my mom, remember."

"Cross my heart, hope to die," I said, drawing a cross on my heart. "No funny stuff." Tom held me for a second longer... and then nodded, letting me pass. I sighed and walked into his house.

Tom's living room was very different from ours. Dad liked things simple. One color on the walls, a few pictures, but not much else. We once tried to put a plant in the corner, but I think it died of boredom. Tom and Sarah's house, though, was like walking into a rainbow. Their lounge was covered in different pieces of art, pictures of Tom and Sarah doing different things together, other pictures of Sarah with people I didn't recognize, paintings, thousands of paintings covering every inch of available space.

It suddenly made sense why Tom complained so much about his house smelling of paint all the time. Sarah was a painter. I had never really thought much about her beyond 'Tom's mom' or 'Dad's kind of girlfriend but he has trouble admitting it'. She was a full on person beyond that simple label. The idea was bewildering.

When she entered the room, she was wearing a long white shirt covered in paint splotches of different colors. Her brown hair was tied back into a hasty ponytail, and she smiled as soon as she saw me.

"Hi, David, hi, Jack," she grinned. "I'd hug you but I'm in the middle of a project at the moment."

Tom looked at me. "I'm sure they'll survive," he said, narrowing his eyes.

15

"Can I get you a cup of coffee? Tea?" Sarah said.

"No, thank you," Dad said. "Me and Ja.... Dad are just popping over to ask you a question."

Sarah raised an eyebrow. "Oh really?"

Tom said, "Oh *reaaaallly?*" and looked at me accusingly. I flashed him an innocent grin.

Dad looked at me.

"Yeah, I mean, whatever, it doesn't really matter, I mean..." I looked around the room. "Nice paintings." Dad, seeing that I was avoiding the question, stepped *politely* on my foot. *Get on with it,* his eyes seemed to say.

"Hmmm." I clenched my teeth to avoid wincing at the pain. "We would like the two of you to...er... come on holiday with us," I said. "To a cabin we have in Memphis."

"Minnesota," Dad coughed into his hand.

"Minnesota," I corrected myself.

"Oh wow, a cabin?" Sarah said, her eyes wide. "What's it like?"

I glanced at Dad who shrugged. "It's next to a lake," I said, as that was the only other piece of information I had about the holiday.

"Yes!" Sarah said excitedly and far too fast. She glanced at Tom guiltily. "I mean if you want to, Tom."

"Yeah, Tom, what do you think?" I asked.

Tom looked between both of us as if he had just been asked the million-dollar question on a TV quiz show.

"Er... yeah?" he said. "Sure? Why not?"

"Brilliant!" Sarah grinned and moved across the room to hug me, but at the last second, she pulled back. "Right, sorry, paint. Paint is bad."

"What are you painting now?" Dad asked, clearly annoyed that she hadn't gone to hug *him*.

"Wanna come upstairs and have a look?" she grinned, before jogging excitedly out of the room.

"I guess we're going upstairs," I said to Dad.

"I'll pass. Painting is *boring*." Tom said, turning on the

games console under the TV. "Wanna game when you come back down?"

"Yeah," I grinned hopefully. "If I can manage it without your mom thinking it's weird!" I hadn't had a proper gaming session with Tom in weeks and I was willing to risk the fact that Sarah would probably think it strange to see me sitting on the couch gaming with her son.

Upstairs, Sarah stood proudly by her work, a large canvas that took up the entire wall of one room. On it were patches of bright colors and some black lines that formed a kind of colourful pattern...but I didn't quite know what it was meant to be.

"What do you think? I call it: Rainbow on canvas."

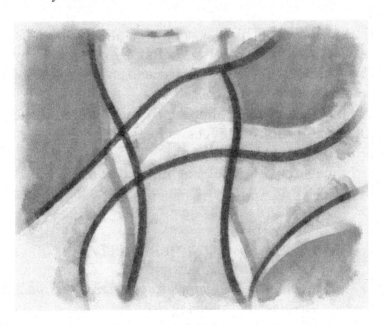

I nodded, turning my head slightly, thinking that it didn't look like a rainbow at all.

"Yeah!" I said. "Well named!"

"Brilliant!" Dad said with a smile.

Sarah punched me in the arm. "You guys are terrible liars," she laughed.

Packing

The next day, Dad waved a piece of paper in front of my face and said, "This is important."

I tried to look around his hand at the TV, as I was deep in a game. "Is this 'homework' important or 'brand new game released' important?" My character in the game let out a scream as he fell down a dark pit. I groaned.

"Homework," said Dad, then his eyebrows lowered. "No, wait... it's a new game. Wait... which is more important, homework or a new game?"

I glanced up at him. "I don't know. What's the game?"

Dad sighed. "This is *very* important, Jack. It's a list of clothes you need to pack for me before we go on holiday in a few days. I know you won't want me to choose the clothes, so you need to do it."

I paused the game after my character tottered over the edge again, letting out yet another scream. Dad was so *distracting*.

I finally took the list from him and scanned it.

JACK'S PACKING LIST
1. *10 pairs of underwear*
2. *10 pairs of socks*
3. *5 pairs of pants (NO JEANS PLEASE)*
4. *2 waterproof coats*
5. *5 pairs of shoes for walking, wet weather, muddy weather and anything else.*
6. *A hat for sunny days*
7. *Two towels*
8. *Swimming trunks*
9. *Toothbrush*

I frowned at the list. "Do I even own ten pairs of socks? And five pairs of pants that *aren't* jeans? I don't know if that is possible."

Dad shrugged. "Maybe we should go shopping then."

I stuck out my tongue. "Ew, no." I picked up a pen from the table, turned his list around and began to write.

"What are you doing?"

"I'm writing *my* list," I said. "You think you can have a list and I can't have a list?"

Dad didn't say anything. He just looked at me with that disapproving look he is so good at (even with my face!). After a few seconds, I handed him back my list. It said:

CLOTHES PLEASE.

I looked up at him and grinned. He rolled his eyes. "Oh, ha, ha."

The next few days were a blur of activity. As I tried to get further and further into my game (that hole was *really* hard to cross! I must have fallen down it at least one thousand times!) Dad rushed around the house, washing clothes, drying them and then folding them up neatly and packing them into his suitcase. Occasionally, his head would pop around the door and he would say, "Have you packed yet?" And I would reply, "Pretty much! Just a little bit more!" and he would be happy and go back to whatever he was doing.

The day before we were due to leave, Tom texted me.

Tom: Wat R we gonna do there?

Me: Dunno. Sumthin awesome.

Tom: Cool

I hadn't seen him this excited in a long time! I decided that maybe it was time to start packing, so I went into my room and started grabbing clothes from my cupboard then shoving them in the suitcase Dad had left on my bed.

They didn't need to be folded because they were going to get creased in the suitcase anyway, right?

The next morning, Dad woke me up by prodding my face.

"Jack," he said. "Get up."

I opened my eyes. It was still dark. I flopped around

19

on the bed like a jellyfish, my arms and legs not quite awake enough to do what I wanted them to.

"Glurb?" My tongue flopped around in my mouth.

"Huh?" said Dad.

"What... what time is it? Is the house on fire?" I mumbled.

"No, we just need to get up now. We have to get to the airport."

The world 'airport' meant something important, but my brain couldn't figure out what it was. I yawned loudly as Dad walked back across the room, stepping over old clothes and tutting at the mess (as he always does when he is in my room). I tried to sit up. Gravity felt very strong this morning, pulling me back down... down to my pillow... my comfy pillow and my warm comforter that wrapped around me like a cloud... and... and...

"WAKE UP," Dad shouted.

My eyes shot open. It was still very dark. Adrenaline kicked my brain into action. "Airport?" I said. "Why do we need to go to the airport?"

"We have to get to Minnesota, remember?" Dad said. "What do you want to do, walk?"

I opened my mouth and closed it again. How far away *was* Minnesota?

"Now, get up!" Dad said. "We are meeting Sarah and Tom at their house in half an hour!"

I rolled out of bed and hit the floor with a *smack*.

"*Uuuuuurgh,*" I groaned.

Forty-seven minutes later, all four of us were standing at the bus stop, staring at the empty road in the darkness. The sun hadn't even risen yet. I yawned loudly. Tom yawned loudly. Sarah and Dad didn't yawn. I suspected them to be robots in disguise. Who *wasn't* tired at this hour?

Sarah and Tom's bags looked a lot newer and nicer than the one I had given to Dad. And they certainly had a lot more stuff.

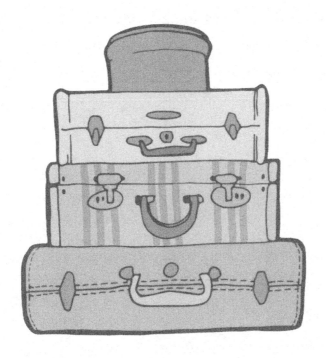

Sarah made it worse by asking Dad: "Is that all you're taking, Jack?"

He looked at me with a frown. "Apparently so."

"Those crazy kids," I joked. "Never packing enough. You'll regret that when we get there, won't you?" I ruffled his hair with my hand in a way that I knew was *very* annoying. He looked at me with eyes that said: *Not as much as you'll regret it!*

I grinned at him. This was my revenge for forcing me to get up so early.

When we were all seated on the bus and it was heading down the road, Sarah moved closer to me. She wrapped her arm around mine and leaned her head on my shoulder. "Are you ready for an adventure?"

Tom shot me a look very similar to the one Dad had

just given me.

I gulped. This was going to be a very long vacation!

At the Airport

As the bus pulled up outside the airport, my mouth dropped open. The airport was like a city in the middle of the city! The sun had risen now, just in time to make the glass building sparkle and shine like no other building I had seen before. Excitement bubbled inside of me. Suddenly, our vacation felt like a proper adventure! I was somewhere new and exciting and I hadn't even left the state yet.

Sarah laughed at me as I pressed my nose against the glass of the building. "You're like a little kid," she grinned. "Come on, let's go inside."

I blushed as she turned away. Was it *that* obvious? I needed to act like an adult around her. An adult who had already seen and done all these things. It was going to be very difficult.

I straightened my back and walked towards the entrance, passing Tom and Dad as I did so.

"Come on, boys," I said in my most adulty voice. "Let's go. Chop chop."

Tom frowned. "Why are you speaking like that?"

"Because I'm an *adult!*" I said, marching around him in a circle.

"Ahh, trying to fool security," he nodded knowingly. "Got it."

As he passed me and entered the building, I tried not to show how terrifying his last few words sounded. Security? It hadn't even occurred to me. Now a big wave of terror came crashing down on me.

Airport security. I had to pretend to be my dad in front of people who were *trained* to spot liars.

As we crossed the airport, dodging travellers from all over the world, coming and going, all dragging suitcases of different shapes and sizes, I felt the nervousness growing inside me. My eyes darted around at the large security men and women who seemed to patrol every corner. They were tall, and looked like they meant business. Their bodies were covered in protective armor, like they expected lions to fall from the sky and attack them at any moment. They could probably have taken me down with the blink of an eye. I was no lion.

I felt a shiver of fear run down my body. *Everything is cool,* I told myself. *Nothing to worry about.* I tried to control my breathing, slow it down and focus on just putting one foot in front of the other.

"Are you alright?" Sarah said, making me jump. "Your knuckles are really white."

I looked down at my hands. They were clamped so tightly around my suitcase handle that almost all the blood had drained from my hand. I took a breath and tried to loosen my fingers, smiling weakly at Sarah. "I just... well... I...."

"Dad's afraid of flying," Dad leaped in to save me. I glanced over at him. I was surprised at *how* quickly he reacted. I nodded.

"Yep. Terrified. Scary. Flying? A big no no."

Sarah smiled warmly. "Aww, don't worry, David. It's only a little flight. It'll be over before you know it." She hugged me and rubbed my back with her free hand. Tom stared at me from behind her with fire in his eyes.

What are you doing? He mouthed.

It's not me, it's her! I mouthed back.

"Did you say something?" Sarah said, pulling back.

"Me? Nope. Tom, did you say something?"

"No," Tom said darkly. "Not yet."

I didn't fail to notice the threat in Tom's eyes. *If you don't leave my mom alone, I'm going to tell her everything.*

I took a few steps away from Sarah, just in case. That was the *last* thing I needed right now.

Everything will be fine, I told myself.

It wasn't. For what felt like the next few hours, we

stood in a queue, watching other people step up to a little desk where a woman in a strange orange uniform sat. She even had a small hat on the side of her head, but I couldn't figure out how it stayed on. She must have been using some kind of hat magic.

But even the mystery of the hat lost interest after a while. Both Tom and I started to get incredibly bored, tapping random beats on our legs, sighing loudly and just staring off into space as the queue crept along like a snail that didn't like to rush things.

"Uuuugh, will this never end?" Tom groaned.

"It feels like we have been here foreverrrrrr," I groaned as well.

Sarah gave me an odd look. Dad shook his head and turned away. I realized I was acting like a kid again.

"I mean..." I quickly stood up straight. "Waiting is good for you, Tom, helps you learn patience and...er... stuff." I nodded knowingly.

"You don't know anything," Tom mumbled, as frustrated as I was.

"Tom!" Sarah looked horrified. "Apologize to David! That was very rude!"

Tom quickly straightened up too. "I'm sorry, Mr. Stevenson," he said through gritted teeth. "I was very rude."

I couldn't help myself from grinning at him. "That's fine, Tom. I, Mr. David Stevenson, knows nothing at all. I am completely brainless."

Tom snorted out a laugh.

"I'm sure you know *some* things, *Dad*," Dad said, his eyes narrowed. "Maybe quite a lot of things. You are a *teacher* after all."

"Nope." I said. "I am like a stupid monkey, OOO OOO AHH AHH!" I started waving my hands around and doing a monkey impression. Tom joined in. Soon we were both pretending to be monkeys in the line at the airport.

"Er... David?" Sarah whispered. "People are looking."

"DAVID WANT BANANA!" I said. Tom laughed out loud. Dad shook his head.

Sarah giggled. "You're a strange man, David Stevenson."

I laughed too, finally feeling calmer. For a second, I had convinced myself that this whole airport situation wasn't as bad as I thought it was.

By then we were next up at the desk, and the fear came back in a massive flood of panic. My palms started sweating. We moved up to the desk and the woman smiled at me.

"Hello Sir. Madam. Do you have your tickets?"

I produced a blue wallet that Dad had put into my backpack and told me was full of the documents we needed. I noticed my hand was visibly shaking. I placed the wallet on the desk in front of me and waited as she took the passports and tickets out of it, one by one. She looked at each ticket, each passport.

Tom's ticket. Tom's passport.

Sarah's ticket. Sarah's passport.

My fingers clenched in my palms.

Dad's ticket. Dad's passport.

I felt a bead of sweat run down my forehead. I wiped it off as quickly as possible.

My ticket.

She looked at it.

She glanced up at me.

She looked at it again.

She typed something into her computer.

I saw a security guard watching us from the side of the room. Was he going to come over and arrest me?

"And you are David Stevenson?" she asked.

"Yep. Yep. That's me. Absolutely me. No one else. That's me. I like Math and I am a teacher and I am very smart and things. I am David Stevenson, yes."

The woman smiled a confused smile at me.

"Very nice. All done," she said. "Place your luggage on the conveyor belt next to me and have a nice flight."

I blinked. That was it? I lifted up my luggage, placed it on the moving belt next to her, and smiled. We all walked out of the queue.

"Well," I said with a big grin. "That was painless! I could do that all day." I felt like a great weight had been lifted off my chest.

"Well, the tough part comes next," Sarah grinned. "Security. Don't look too suspicious!" She laughed loudly and happily as the great weight landed back onto my chest with a thud. It wasn't over.

"Heh, yeah," I said quietly.

I laughed too, but inside I felt like I could dissolve at any second. My legs were jelly.

We joined yet another queue, but this one was shorter. At the end of this queue wasn't a friendly looking woman sitting at a desk, but a big, mean looking man who scowled at everyone who got too close. He stood on the other side of a big, metal machine that people had to walk through when he told them to step forward. It must have been the metal detectors I always heard about. All around us were big signs that said things like:

NO MORE THAN 100ML OF LIQUID
MAKE SURE YOU REMOVE ALL METAL ITEMS
DO WHAT YOU ARE TOLD BY SECURITY PERSONNEL

It was like school, only a thousand million times worse. Everything looked terrifying. I was terrified.

Slowly we inched forward and Sarah started sorting out Tom, making him take off his jacket and shoes. I frowned, and glanced at Dad who nodded in their direction and indicated that I should probably do the same. I removed my backpack, the old jacket and uncomfortable shoes that Dad had made me wear, and placed them into a box on the conveyor belt. I was last again, forced to watch Sarah, Tom and Dad walk through the machine one by one on a nod from the beastly looking security guard who stood on the other side.

I watched my backpack disappear into the machine. I tried to remember what I had put inside it. Was there anything dangerous? I didn't think so, but suddenly my mind was a blur.

"Step forward sir," the security guard said without a hint of a smile. He wore a white shirt and black trousers, but his muscles bulged with a ferocious anger underneath it. I imagined that if he wanted to, he could squash me with one hand. I closed my eyes and stepped through the machine and...

BEEP BEEP BEEP BEEP!

I panicked and looked around. What had I done? What was going on? Should I run? I didn't want to be squashed! I looked at Dad, who grinned at me. Why was he grinning?

The security guard stood close to me and grimaced. He started waving a small machine around my body. It hummed as it passed my face and went down my chest. As it hit my waist, it went, 'EEEEEEE'.

I looked down. *What* did I have on myself that would make it go EEEE?

"Lift up your shirt," the guard commanded.

I glanced at him, worried, and then lifted up my shirt.

The security guard shook his head. "Your belt, sir. It set off the machine."

I looked down at my trousers. I was wearing a belt with a metallic buckle. Of course! That was what had set off the machine. I grinned helplessly at the security guard.

"Sorry?" I said.

"Move on," the guard grunted.

Flying out of Control

After that, it was smooth sailing. We sat in a restaurant and had lemonade until it was time to board the plane. After standing in yet another queue, we were pushed onto a small plane which smelled a bit like cheese. I was squeezed in the back, between an extraordinarily fat man and Tom. He had persuaded Sarah that he wanted to sit by me so we could 'bond'. She seemed to love that idea! Somewhere else on the plane, she sat with Dad. Getting tickets next to each other was apparently impossible.

Tom sniggered as he saw that the fat man had *already* fallen asleep and was using me as a pillow.

"This is going to be fun," I groaned. I could feel the blood seeping out of my arm.

The plane's engine started off as a rumble, and then grew to a roar as we sped up the runway. I grinned at Tom and he grinned back at me as we felt the wheels lift off from the ground. We were flying! I felt a rush of adrenaline as we pulled higher and higher into the sky, and my ears popped as the pressure changed. I really loved flying.

Truth be told, I felt a lot better being a fat man's pillow than being harassed by the security guards. Tom and I were settling down to a good gaming session on his Game Kid Ultra 3D when there was a commotion further up the plane. I tried to look over the seats to see who it was, but I could already tell. I rolled my eyes. Dad was causing trouble again.

I sat up straighter, nudging the fat man's head away, so it clonked against the plane window, and tried to listen as best I could.

"I just... I just need to breathe..."

"Madam, could you control your son? He is stepping on my dress! This is a Chanel dress! Do you *know how much this cost?*"

Three rows in front of us, I could see Dad climbing between the seats trying to get out into the aisle. He seemed to be standing *on* the seats, climbing from his, next to the window and onto the unfortunate woman's seat next to him! The woman tried to bat him away with her hand, but failed. A hostess walked over, her orange uniform similar to that of the woman who had served us at the desk.

"Sir, could you please sit down? The seat belt signs have not yet been turned off..."

I groaned. Why could it not just be an easy flight?

"You don't understand," Dad said, breathlessly. "I can't breathe properly in this plane, I need to just walk around and..."

"Sir, we need you to sit down, or we are going to have to land the plane. Sir, sit down, please."

My eyes widened. Dad *was* afraid of flying! I thought that was just a joke he made up to stop me from looking stupid, but here he was panicking! He needed something to calm him down fast. I looked around the plane. Other people were watching, some were laughing. It was *so embarrassing.*

Sarah reached up from her seat. "Jack, Jack, calm down," she said. "It'll all be OK."

"No, you don't understand," Dad replied, trying to step forward again and making the woman between them squeak a bit more. "I'm not Jack, I don't..."

Oh no! Dad is going to tell Sarah if I don't do something soon. I looked frantically around me for something to help calm Dad down or make him stop. On the lap of the fat man next to me, there was an open packet of sweets. Tom leaned over me and looked at the sweets as well.

"That might get his attention," he grinned.

I snatched the packet of sweets off the fat man's legs with a little apology (he didn't hear anyway, he just continued snoring) and took the first, round red sweet in my hand, holding it between my first finger and my thumb.

I sighed. "Well, here goes nothing." How hard could it be?

I aimed at Dad and threw it across the seats in front of me. It missed Dad and hit an old lady in the back of the head. Oops. Turns out throwing sweets is not as easy as throwing a football.

"Oh, heavens!" she said, turning around to see what had hit her.

I ducked and looked at Tom, who cringed and snorted a laugh. "You hit her really hard!" he hissed.

"Shh!" I snapped, standing up again. "That was a practice throw."

"Sir, you really need to..." The air hostess turned as something hit her on the shoulder. Something small and green. She frowned, but then turned back to Dad.

"You're rubbish at this," Tom chuckled.

"I don't see *you* helping!" I said.

Tom held out his hand. "Gimme some. I want a go."

I reluctantly held out the packet of sweets and Tom took a handful. He aimed and threw one.

It rattled off a nearby wall. I snorted with laughter. Tom growled and snatched another sweet, aiming again.

The passengers of the plane were starting to wonder where all the sweets came from when I finally struck Dad on the cheek. He was balanced between two armrests, his face squished against the air vent as he tried to climb over the seat.

He frowned and looked down the plane, right at me.

From deep inside me, I summoned the teacher voice that I had been using over the last few weeks. I didn't like it, but it was effective.

"SIT. DOWN," I said through gritted teeth. Even Tom shuddered when I used it.

Dad paused, thought about it and then climbed down, back into his chair again. He mumbled a "sorry" to the woman beside him, who was still ranting to Sarah about her dress.

A few people on the plane applauded. The air hostess looked at me with relief. I sat back down with a sigh.

Tom gave me a strange look.

"What?" I asked.

Tom shook his head. "How did you do that voice?" he asked.

I shrugged. "Don't know. I just call it the 'teacher voice'. I had to use it in school a few times, and Dad uses it all the time."

"That's creepy," Tom said. "Do you ever think that maybe you swapped *more* than just bodies?"

"What do you mean?" I asked.

"I'm just saying," he shrugged. "You seemed more like the parent there and Mr. Stevenson was more like... you know... us.... I don't know..." Tom thought about it. "Like a kid, I guess."

I opened my mouth to reply, but couldn't think of anything to say. *More* than just bodies?

Lying on the Ground

When we finally got out of the plane, it felt like we were finally free of a prison that we had been trapped in for hours. No one looked more relieved to be off the plane than Dad, and as we passed the air hostess on the way out, she waved us off with a very fake smile. I think she was glad to see the back of us, too.

We all filled our lungs with the fresh(ish) air of the new airport, which was a *lot* smaller than the previous one, and headed towards the luggage collection point. As we watched the conveyor belt spin around and around with luggage of all different shapes and sizes, I took Dad to one side and whispered to him: "So, you're afraid of flying. Didn't think of mentioning that *before* we got on the plane?"

Dad sniffed. "I thought I would have gotten over it by now. It's been years since I last flew."

"You haven't," I pointed out.

"I haven't," Dad agreed.

"Anything else you're not telling me?" I closed my eyes. I think I had a headache coming on.

Dad picked up his suitcase as it tried to roll past him. "Well, about the next part of the journey..."

"All good?" Sarah interrupted us. "I managed to grab your suitcase too, David," she smiled and offered me the ancient brown thing from under Dad's bed.

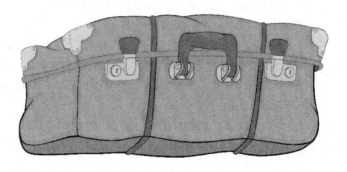

"Thanks," I said, taking it and praying it would disintegrate and we'd have to spend the next few hours picking Dad's underwear off the floor.

She looked at us both, suitcases in hand. "Brilliant! We can go and get the car then."

"Yes," I said. "The car." I glanced towards Dad. I had no idea what she was talking about. Sarah set off in a brisk stride, humming pleasantly to herself. The rest of us had to jog to keep up. Tom yawned loudly.

"How can she have so much energy after that flight?" he groaned.

It soon became clearer where we were going. We followed Sarah out of the main building, along a walking path crowded with people, and into another smaller building that had a bright green sign over the top. It said:

CAR RENTALS

As we were about to go inside, Dad grabbed me by the arm and hissed: "You can't drive, Jack. You've got to think of an excuse."

"Why did you *rent a car* if you didn't want me to drive?"

"Well technically, Sarah rented it," Dad said, as if that made it better. "There's no other way to get to the cabin. I thought we could get her to drive. You have to pretend you're feeling ill or something."

I scowled at him. I remembered the good old days when Dad told me that *lying was wrong* and that it *hurt people*. Now he just wanted me to lie all the time. I racked my brains but they were too tired to come up with something worthwhile. Sarah talked to the man at the desk and began to fill out some forms. I slumped next to Tom in a plastic chair by the window.

"I've got an idea," Tom said. "I know how to get you out of driving the car."

"Yeah?" I grinned.

"Yeah," he said. "It's fool proof. Just follow my lead."

I nodded. At least *Tom* was trying. Dad was just standing by the doorway nervously rubbing his hands together.

Finally, after another long wait, the man behind the desk handed Sarah some keys. "I hope you're ready to drive us," Sarah told me with a grin, then turned towards the parking lot. We gathered our belongings and followed her out. She was trying to find the car, looking for space H165, when Dad suddenly squeaked: "He can't drive!"

"Why not?" Sarah said with a frown.

"He's...er... well..." Dad tried to think of something.

"Drunk!" Tom chimed in. I turned towards him, wide-eyed, and he winked at me. "Completely drunk off his face. I saw him drink three of those little bottles on the plane. I told him to stop and that it wasn't good for him, Mom, but he wouldn't listen." Tom shook his head at me and I tried to resist the urge to strangle him right there.

DRUNK? THAT WAS HIS BRILLIANT IDEA? I realized that Tom was, again, trying to sabotage my relationship with his mom. By the way she was looking at me, almost shocked by the news, I wondered if he had actually managed to do it.

"Is this... true, David?" she said quietly.

I looked between grinning Tom and silently pleading Dad. They both wanted me to say yes for completely different reasons. After a long, loud sigh, I turned towards her. "It's true," I nodded, although the lie tasted like dirt in my mouth. "I am drunk. Completely. I am in no condition to drive. I didn't think, I'm sorry."

Sarah shook her head. "No, you didn't think." Her words stung. "Alright, I'll drive then."

With that, she stormed off towards the location of the car, leaving us all standing there.

"Oooooh," Tom whispered. "You're in trooouble."

"No thanks to you," I hissed back. "I'm drunk? Really?"

36

Tom shrugged. "You're not driving, are you?" He bounced off after Sarah with a spring in his step. I growled and followed him, leaving Dad to bring up the rear.

We found the car we had rented on the other side of the parking lot. Tom whistled. "That is a *big* car," he said. He wasn't lying either. The car was at least twice the size of the one we had at home, and three times the size of Sarah's. She looked at it worriedly. "Are you sure we have the right one?" she asked.

I looked down at the piece of paper in her hand. The name of the car on it was an

UBER GRAND SUPER TRAVELLER DELUXE EXTREME.

I looked at the car. Those same words shone on the door in a bright silver. I nodded. "Looks like it."

Sarah sighed. "Alright then." She turned towards me. "You can sit in the back, David, and sleep off the alcohol." She twisted on her heels and opened the front door of the car, getting in. She slammed the door closed.

Tom grimaced. "Ouch, that looked painful." I stood blushing in the parking lot.

"You're enjoying this too much," I said. Tom nodded with a big grin on his face.

I sat in the back of the car with Tom, and there was still enough room left for a whole party with dancing and a DJ booth. "Wow," I said, "This is amazing," stretching my legs out. It made a nice change from the cramped plane.

"Shouldn't you be asleep?" Sarah snapped and turned on the engine. It rumbled to life like a dragon waking from a deep sleep.

I decided to close my eyes, just to make her feel a bit happier. I secretly hoped that she would forgive me by the time we reached the cabin.

To my surprise, when I next opened my eyes, the scenery outside had changed dramatically. I must have fallen asleep without realizing it! We were far from the city, on a long winding road surrounded by tall pine trees. Even the air smelled fresher and cleaner. I stared out the window in astonishment, trying to take it all in. I listened to Sarah talking to Dad in the front of the car.

"Does your dad usually drink like this, Jack?" she asked.

Dad didn't answer right away. "No, he doesn't. Never, really."

"I'm just worried about him," she said. "I mean, do you think he is uncomfortable with me or..."

"No," Dad said. "Not at all. I think he is just nervous. He wants to make a good impression on you and got a bit carried away. Like at the dinner party."

A few weeks earlier, we had had a dinner party where I had drunk wine (by accident...! And then I had a bit more). The results weren't great, but it turns out Sarah was surprisingly forgiving, even when I stumbled about her house all night.

"Oh," she replied. It sounded like she was smiling.

At the Cabin

When my eyes opened next, someone was shaking my shoulders. "Wake uuuup, lazy bones!" Tom shouted in my ear.

I mumbled and sniffed, wiping the drool off my cheek and tried to bat him away like he was an annoying fly. "Why are you so *loud*?" I grumbled.

Tom grinned. "Because we're *here*! We made it to the cabin."

I turned to look out the car door, and squinted as sunlight blinded me. Protecting my eyes with my hand, I could make out a muddy path, surrounded by tall pine trees which led up to the wooden cabin I remembered from the picture. It sat waiting for us, overgrown with shrubs that hadn't been trimmed in years.

I unclipped my seatbelt and stepped outside the car, stretching my legs and arms. Dad, by the front of the car, was doing something similar. "Ahhh," he said. "That's more like it. This place is exactly how I remember it."

Sarah frowned as she passed him to the trunk of the car. "How old were you when you last came here, Jack?"

"Twenty-ei..." Dad stopped mid-sentence. "Two and a half. I just have a really good memory," he added quickly.

"Apparently so," Sarah said.

I decided it was time to check out the cabin. I took a step forward and-

SQUELCH.

"Aww gross!" I said, looking down at Dad's sneakers on my feet. I had trodden right into a deep, muddy puddle. Cold water began to seep into my socks.

"Oh, yeah, look out for that," Tom laughed. I shot him a scowl and tried to recover as much of my foot as possible, but it was too late. I shivered as the mud dripped deeper into my shoe.

I attempted to pull myself free, but somehow I felt my feet sink further into the mud. I pulled on one of my feet and it came out with a *plop!* Then I gently placed it down on the dry ground in front of me. Then. I. struggled. to. pull. out. the. other. fooooooooooot. PLOP.

I almost fell forward when the mud finally let me go. Stumbling towards the cabin, I grabbed hold of Tom's shoulder to stabilize myself. His whole body shook as he laughed at me.

"Thanks, Tom," I said coldly.

Tom grinned at me, and I could hear Sarah and Dad chuckling too from the other side of the car.

"Can we just go *inside*?" I sighed. The steps of the cabin beckoned. As I got closer, I realized that the place had definitely seen better days. The steps alone were broken and cracked, a strange green moss was growing up the posts that held up the roof and the windows were covered in dust and spider webs. I walked up to the door, each piece of wood creaking as I did so, and tested the handle. It was locked.

"Do you have the key, D... er... Jack?" I asked.

Dad began searching in his backpack. "Yeah, I've got it here somewhere. Let me just..."

"Helloooooooo!" A deep, booming voice made us all turn and look up. A large man in square framed glasses and a red shirt jogged down the dirt track towards us.

"Oh, yeah," Dad mumbled as if he was remembering something that was probably vitally important. I was right.

"David!" shouted the man with a big grin. "It's been *years*, buddy! How have you been?"

The big man crossed through the mud like it was nothing and held out his arms wide.

"Er.. Hi," I said just as the man wrapped his arms around me in a big bear hug.

"I never thought I'd see you again!" he chuckled loudly into my ear.

"Ack... ack... aaaack!" I said, desperately trying to

41

breathe. He *finally* released me and looked at me with a smile. I took in a long, soothing breath. Ahhh oxygen!

"The old cabin's in rough shape, eh?" He patted a wooden post, looked at his hand and then wiped it on his pants. "She's seen better days, that's for sure, but you'll get her back up and running in no time, eh? I think the generator still works round back. I've tested it a few times over the years." The man talked and talked with a big smile but I still had no idea who he was.

"Er... thanks," I said. "It's good to see you too." I tapped him on the shoulder and smiled. "It has been too long."

The man smiled wider. "Come round the cabin tomorrow, Stacy would love to see you again. Especially since..." The man's voice trailed off. "Well, you know." I really had no idea, but I nodded anyway. The man turned and saw Sarah standing by the car. It set him off again. "And she would love to meet your new friends!" He marched over to Sarah and also gave her a hug.

"Welcome to Pine Valley!" he said. "You are?"

Sarah recovered her breath and wheezed. "Sarah... And that's Tom."

Tom waved and ducked behind the car, wisely hiding from the hugs.

"I'm Greg!" I made a mental note to remember the name. Greg. Crazy hugging man's name was Greg. "I hope you have a fantastic time here! And YOU!" Greg turned his sights onto Dad. "You must be JACK! Wow, you've grown so big."

Dad nodded. "I have, haven't I?"

Greg held out his arms and squeezed. Dad, somehow, was prepared and managed to squeeze right back.

"Wow!" Greg said. "This guy knows how to do a Pine Valley greeting! You've taught him well, David!"

I smiled weakly, hoping my lungs hadn't been crushed beyond repair, and nodded.

"I'll see you all later! Have a great stay!" And like that, he was gone, marching off back up the road the way he came.

"Wow," I said. "That was..."

"That man sure knows how to hug," Sarah laughed, from her spot behind us.

Dad handed me the key to the cabin and whispered quietly, "Sorry about that, I forgot about Greg and his rather intense hugs. If you hug him back though, they aren't so bad." He rubbed his chest. Maybe he hadn't managed to avoid the worst of it after all.

I turned the key in the lock. There was a soft click. "Clearly you remembered enough to keep your lungs intact," I whispered back. "We just need to..." I stepped into the cabin and looked around. Something in the back of my mind sparked in recognition. Of old times, long ago. I recognized the now faded carpet on the floor that was red and had elephants on it. I recognized the mirror at the other end of the hall. In it, Dad's face stared back at me.

Aaaaa CHOO! I sneezed.

"Phew," I said. "This place needs airing out."

I took a few more steps inside.

"That's one bedroom," Dad pointed at a closed door next to us as he headed quickly through the house ahead of Sarah and Tom. "And the other bedroom is there."

"Cool," I said, stepping over to the nearest door. "Let's have a look at this room th-"

I stopped talking. My mouth dropped open as I stared into the room. "Dad," I hissed. "What is *that?*"

The Picture

In the center of the room sat a double bed. The mattress looked like it had survived quite well over the years it had been abandoned, but that wasn't the point. The point was that it was a *double* bed. A double bed that I would have to share with *Sarah*. My throat tightened. This wasn't good. Apart from the fact that Tom would probably explode and try to murder me, I would have to *share* a bed with *Sarah*. That would be super weird!

"Ah, I'd forgotten about that!" Dad said. "Yes, that is a problem."

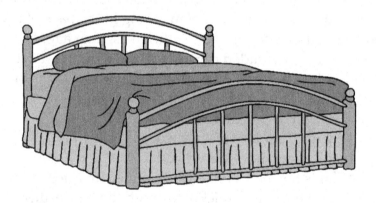

"What's a problem?" Sarah asked.

I slammed the door closed before she could look inside and then spun around. Sarah stood in the doorway, holding two suitcases in her hands.

"Nothing!" I said quickly. "Nothing at all. Everything is great. Greater than great. Super great. Your bedroom is down the hall." I smiled sweetly and Sarah frowned and nodded slowly. She pulled the cases behind her down the corridor. When she went into the other room, I turned back to Dad. "What are we going to *do*?" I hissed.

"I guess we're sharing a bed," Dad grimaced.

I sighed. I had to *share* with *Dad?* Ugh. This holiday was getting worse and worse by the second. I just wanted to chill out for a week, but now I realized that it was going to be a lot more difficult than that.

"Are you *sure* this is my room?" Sarah shouted from the other end of the cabin.

"Yep, absolutely. Isn't it great?" I said quickly.

"Stop saying *great*," Dad whispered.

"But there's only one bed in here," Sarah's voice came again from the bedroom.

"Great," I groaned. "I mean... fantastic." I shot another angry glance at Dad, who looked guilty.

"There's a bed under the sofa," Dad chimed in quickly. He glanced at me. "That is where Tom is sleeping."

"Ahhh," Sarah said, emerging from the room.

Tom stood in the doorway. "I'm sleeping on the floor? How is *that* fair?" he said.

"Do you want me sharing a bed with your mom?" I hissed.

"The floor can actually be surprisingly comfy," Tom quickly agreed. He disappeared back into the living room.

Dad wandered into the bedroom and started rummaging through the cupboard. He told me to get our bags from the car. After all, my shoes were already caked in mud, so what would a little more do?

I grumbled and groaned and grumbled as I wandered over to the car and got our bags out of the trunk. I had to hold them up so they wouldn't drag along the ground and get muddy in the process. By the time I reached the cabin again, my arms were aching. I breathed out heavily as Sarah walked past me again.

"You need to work out more," she grinned. "Keep going, big guy."

I was breathing too heavily to reply. Maybe I *did* need to work out more. This old guy body was getting annoying.

With one final effort, I dragged the bags inside and

opened the door to the bedroom. "You know," I said between breaths. "You could help me."

Dad was sitting on the bed holding a picture frame in his hands. He didn't seem to hear what I said, and just continued to stare at it.

"Dad?" I said. "Earth to Daaaaad?"

The door closed behind me and I sat on the bed next to him. "What are you looking at?"

I looked at the picture in Dad's hands. It showed my two year old self, wearing a ridiculous hat and sunglasses far too big for my toddler head. I was in a woman's arms, and she too was smiling, her face warm and happy as she stared at me lovingly. Her face was partially obscured by the sweeping brown hair that covered half of her face, but I could see enough to know that she was beautiful. I recognized that face, but I hadn't seen a picture of her in years.

Something caught in my throat.

"Is that Mom?" I whispered.

Dad swallowed and then put the picture on the bed, facing downward.

"I found it in the wardrobe," he said in a quiet voice. "I forgot about all of this."

"Why would you hide the pictures away?" I asked.

"It's..." Dad took another breath. "It's in the past. We need to move on."

In the past. It suddenly clicked in my brain why we hadn't come back to the cabin in so many years. The last time we had been here was with Mom, just before she died. I had been so young, it hadn't really affected me, but Dad – for Dad it was all there. Still fresh in his memory.

"We can't just *move on*, Dad," I said, my voice rising more than I expected. "That's Mom. You can't just pretend she never existed!"

Dad stood up. "You don't..." he began in a shout, but then lowered his voice. "You don't understand, Jack. You were too young. It was difficult."

"Well, tell me then!" I said. "I'm old enough now."

"No," Dad said. "I.... I can't." He walked towards the door and opened it, storming out of the room.

"Dad!" I called after him.

By the time I reached the doorway, and looked out of the cabin, Dad had already left. He was stalking down the road away from the cabin, and back towards where – I assumed – Greg lived. I was going to chase after him, but something made me turn back and look into the room.

He had taken the picture with him. A small part of me wondered if I would ever get to see it again. Anger suddenly rose up in me. *Let him go,* I thought to myself. *He just wants to hide everything from me, as always.*

"Are you OK?" Sarah stood at the door. "You look pale as a sheet. Was that Jack storming off out there?"

No. I thought. Wouldn't it be easier if we just told her everything? Yet something made me hold my tongue. "Yes, he is a bit upset. Let him walk it off."

Sarah nodded. "I understand. Do you know where the generator is? We should probably get some power on in here. It's getting dark."

I glanced at the window. "It's around the back," I said, remembering Greg's words. "I'll go have a look at it now."

"Thanks, David," she said.

Yeah, I grumbled to myself, *thanks a lot, David.*

Finding the Generator

It was dark around the back of the cabin. I could hear the wind whistling through the trees, and those weird bugs that make that creaking sound at night. Compared to home, it was like a completely different world. I stood and looked across the lake for a while, lights sparkling in the distance. I tried to make out what they were, but it was too far. Probably some kind of building, maybe a house, I decided.

I got to what I assumed was the power generator. It was a hulking beast that smelled a lot like a gas station, only much, much worse. I held my phone up as a makeshift torch, and that was when I truly realized how terrible a torch my phone was.

The generator was a metal contraption with bits of plastic all over it. Tubes and wires were stuck in on every side in a way that made no sense. I quickly came to the conclusion that I had no idea what I was doing, and should probably wait for Dad to get back from his little walk.

But when *would* he be coming back?

No, I thought. I am the adult here now. I can figure this out.

A twig snapped under my foot and it made me jump. I laughed and rolled my eyes at the sky. This was stupid. How hard could it be?

I glanced at my phone. No signal. I doubted there was WI FI anywhere either. No chance of looking up the answers on the internet. I was going to have to figure this one out on my own. I studied the top of the generator. There was something that looked like somewhere to pour stuff in, and there were two buttons, too. A green one and a red one on the top. I shrugged. Green means go, I thought to myself. Surely I just had to press the button and everything would be fixed, right?

My brain agreed. Go brain power! I had a mental

image of the generator blowing up in my face. I mentally made a note to stop watching so many action movies.

I closed my eyes and pushed the button.

There was a growl, a roar from the machine that made me step back a little. Then it settled into a soft 'chug-a-chug' before the lights in the cabin flickered on. There was a cheer from inside.

"Woo!" I threw my arms up in the air. "Jack One, Generator zero!"

As if in response to my celebration, the generator suddenly stopped making a noise with a quiet hisssssss and the lights flickered out in the cabin again.

I lowered my arms. "Fine," I groaned. "Jack one, generator, one. But this isn't over!"

I realized that I was talking to an inanimate object. That probably wasn't a good sign. I turned around and looked back at the lake. The lights on the other side taunted me with their ability to turn on.

I leaned on the generator and sighed. It was clear that I had no idea what I was doing. I was going to have to wait for Dad to get back.

My hand itched. I frowned and brushed it with my other hand. My hand continued to itch. It was very annoying. I stared down at it. I couldn't see anything in the darkness. Bringing up my phone, I looked at the offending hand to see what was wrong with it.

I quickly wished I hadn't.
My hand was covered in hundreds of little red spiders from the nest I had accidentally disturbed. They were crawling all over me!

"Argh!" I screamed, shaking my hand and trying to get them off me. Suddenly, my whole body was itchy beyond belief. They were all over me! "Argh! Get them off! Get them off!" I started dancing around in a little circle, trying to pat down my whole body. I couldn't see anything except little red spiders everywhere.

"David?" Sarah had come out to see what all the noise was about.

"Spiders!" I shouted. "All over my body!"

"Oh no! I hope they aren't the biting type!" Sarah said, holding a hand in front of her mouth and looking around at the floor. The *biting* type? I hadn't even considered that. A whole new level of fear swept through my body, and I launched myself towards the lake.

"David?" Sarah called after me.

I didn't hear her, I was deaf with fear and the itching was going crazy all over my body. I didn't think. I just acted on instinct. It wasn't long before I was running down a little wooden pier, the timber decking thumping under my feet. I ran and I ran until there was no more pier and that was when a little voice in my head said:

Hmm. Maybe this wasn't the smartest plan.

"Davi-!" Sarah screamed.

SPLOOSH!!!

It was even darker in the water, and there was complete silence except for a quiet ringing in my ears. Then I realized how cold it was. Icy cold. I wanted to kick my legs and swim back to the surface, but they were too sluggish to respond. It was like getting out of bed in the morning, except I couldn't breathe and I was freezing cold. My hands tried to grab for something, anything to pull myself out, but all that surrounded me was darkness.

At least you got rid of the spiders, the little voice in my head taunted.

I kicked and kicked again, but I sank further and further into the lake. I realized that if I didn't do something soon, this was going to be the end of Jack Stevenson, most handsome boy in the world.

I was going to drown.

The little voice in my head perked up again with its last comment on the situation.

Worst. Vacation. Ever.

Out of the Lake

The lake was deep and the lake was cold. The further down I sank, the darker the world became. I needed to think of a way out of this, and fast. I was pretty sure that I had seen this exact scene in a movie once. I closed my eyes and tried to think of how the hero of that tale got out of the water.

A *jetpack*. He had used a jetpack to blast himself out of the water.

I realized that maybe I watched too much TV. It wasn't going to help me this time.

My legs seemed to have given up completely now. They felt like lead weights, dragging me deeper and deeper into the water. My arms were definitely going the same way. The water wrapped around me like the world's coldest blanket and the last bubbles of air popped out of my mouth, floating to the surface.

"You're just going to give up?"

My eyes opened. Floating in front of me in the water was my girlfriend, Holly.

I frowned. *She* wasn't having any trouble moving around in the water. She wasn't having any trouble speaking, either.

"Come on, Jack," she said. "You can't just sink down to the bottom of the lake. It is *gross* down here. I mean, look at that!" She pointed at some trash that floated by. "If you want to see me again, you're going to have to kick."

I pathetically attempted to kick my legs. They wobbled a bit.

"Harder!" she shouted. "Get moving!"

I kicked again, and again. Slowly, I began to rise.

"It's about time." She rolled her eyes.

Wow, I thought. *My underwater visions of Holly are really judgmental.*

Then it happened. Hands grabbed my arms and pulled. Holly was helping me out of the water.

When I finally reached the surface and felt myself dragged back onto the end of the dock, the world lurched back into life in an explosion of sound. The wind rushed through my hair, the trees creaked, birds sang and the world exploded in color. Everything was blurry and spun around me. I heard a distant voice, as if it was at the end of a tunnel. A long tunnel.

"Holly?" I mumbled.

Then she was over me. "It's OK, I've got you," she whispered to me, her damp blond hair dripping on me. "You're safe now."

"Holly," I tried to say, but all I could feel was water filling my mouth still. Holly leaned forward, our faces almost touching.

"It's OK," she said again. "I'll save you, buddy." I frowned. *Buddy?* But that was all washed away as she leaned in close, our lips almost touching as her beard tickled my chin...

HOLD UP. Rough skin? Unshaved cheeks?

My eyes opened, for real this time. Greg was leaning

over me, his mouth pressing hard against mine. He breathed disgusting, hot air into my mouth. Horror took over. I wriggled and pushed him back off me, my lungs drawing in a long, desperate breath. My mouth tasted like garlic. I spat out onto the floor. I just *knew* that I would be tasting Greg for weeks. *Gross.*

Sarah stood behind him and clapped her hands. "You saved him!" she said with a big grin. "Oh thank goodness, I was so worried!"

"Those first aid classes sure came in handy!" Greg grinned. "I never thought I'd have to do the kiss of life on someone, but here you are, alive!"

"Did you *really* have to do the kiss off life?" I asked, scraping my tongue on the back of my hand. It tasted like lake water, so it wasn't much better.

"Well, you're alive, aren't you?" Greg patted me on the back.

"I am, I guess. Thanks."

"Not a problem, buddy!" Greg stood up. "I was just coming round to bring you this." He pointed at a steaming apple pie that lay on the dock next to us. "Stacy made it fresh this evening for you all. That's when I heard the splashing and commotion."

"Sorry, I'm a bit of a screamer," Sarah smiled with embarrassment. "Why did you jump in the lake, David?" she asked, the concern still on her face.

I shrugged. "I just wondered how deep it was. Turns out, it's pretty deep."

Both Greg and Sarah stared at me for a second, and then Greg burst out in a loud, hearty laugh.

"David, you crazy fool," he smiled. "Good to know you haven't lost that famous sense of humor!"

As Greg helped me to my feet, I tried to picture Dad as a 'crazy fool'. 'Boring teacher' was a much better description. Or maybe 'snore-inducing adult'. *Famous sense of humor?* Dad didn't have a sense of humor, never mind a *famous* one! I just nodded and smiled as if I had an idea what he was talking about. I wondered if he was confusing me with *another* David that he knew. It was possible.

Sarah wrapped her arms around me. *"Don't* do that again," she said in a way that suggested she would do much worse things than try to drown me if I did.

"OK, I promise," I said, hugging her back. Don't get any ideas now, I didn't hug her in a weird 'I like to hug Sarah and I want her to be my girlfriend' kind of way. No, I hugged her because I suddenly realized how *cold* I was. My teeth were chattering as I shook in her warm embrace.

"David," she said, her eyes wide and worried. "You're shivering!"

Greg patted me on the back with a huge hand. "You get inside; I'll get this generator working. Last thing we want is you jumping in the lake again!" As he gave another barking laugh. I nodded and failed to stop my body from twitching. I wasn't planning on going back towards the lake for a while.

Sarah almost dragged me back into the cabin. The first thing she did when we were inside was throw a towel at me and give me strict instructions to get changed. I peeled the wet, smelly clothes off in my bedroom and changed into the comfiest pair of pajamas I could find. Making a mental note to buy myself a jetpack if I ever got the chance, I wrapped the comforter around me and walked into the living room like a big fluffy ghost. Tom was lying on the couch.

"You *jumped into the lake?!"* Tom said as I recounted what had happened. I decided to leave out the bit where Greg kissed me (I did brush my teeth about 200 times later though).

"Not my smartest move," I said. "It's pretty dark down there in the water, and cold. Very, very cold."

"Yeah, your lips are like purple," Tom said, poking my face.

I knocked his hand away.

"But, while you were swimming," he continued. "I found something weird here in the cabin."

I rolled my eyes. "*Please* don't tell me it's haunted. The last thing I need now is a pesky ghost chasing us around."

"*I ain't afraid of no ghost!*" Tom grinned. "But no, it isn't. Look at this!" Tom stood up and walked over to a cupboard in the corner. Opening the doors, he produced a guitar and a small black book. "I didn't know your dad played guitar."

I frowned. "He doesn't." Then it clicked. I swallowed. That was my *mom's* guitar.

"And look at this," Tom said, resting the guitar against the sofa. "It's a photo album filled with..."

The sound of the cabin door opening interrupted us.

"Anyone home?" Dad asked. Tom looked at me and a silent communication passed between us. Tom picked up the guitar, putting it back in the cupboard, and I slid the album under the sofa. We could look at it later.

Dad entered the room. "What's up?" he said. I didn't look at him and he didn't look at me. A silent agreement was made that we weren't going to talk about what had happened earlier. It was a Stevenson thing.

"You came back just in time!" Sarah said, emerging from the kitchen. "Greg brought pie!"

"Ooh, pie!" Dad said, smiling.

Tom glanced at me. This was going to be a *long* holiday.

A long night

SNOOOOORRRREEEEE.

I stared at the wooden ceiling of the cabin, silently wishing that someone would tear my ears off.

SNNNNNNOOOOOOOOREEE. SNORT. SNNOOOOORRRE.

The snoring had begun about ten minutes after Dad had fallen asleep, and hadn't stopped since. I had been lying in the bed for about three hours now.

SNNOOOOREEEEE. SNOREY SNOOOOOORE.

I tried to distract myself by thinking about my mom's picture, about the guitar, and how little I knew about her. It occurred to me that Dad had held back a lot of information. I knew so little of her that she was almost a stranger, and yet there was still a small piece of my heart that *begged* to know more. What she was like, what she thought of me, what her favorite food was. Anything. I needed to find a way to get Dad to tell me more about her.

SNNNOOOOREE GLLABBLE SNOOORE.

But that wasn't going to happen tonight. The only thing coming out of Dad's mouth tonight was a sound that reminded me of an angry chainsaw.

I tried turning away from him. I tried wrapping a pillow around my head. I even tried kicking him in the leg. Nothing seemed to end the violent roar of his throat. Soon I just lay there staring at him in disbelief. How could a noise like *that* come out of someone's throat? Come out of *my* throat?

SNNNNORRT. GRUMBLE.

It was the *worst*. I wasn't going to get any sleep at this rate. I lay back on the bed with the smell of unfamiliar bedclothes and unfamiliar cabin in my nose. Had this really been the awesome place in my childhood that the picture suggested? It was hard to imagine anything fun happening here.

The most fun I've had here so far is nearly drowning, I thought to myself. *Did I really have fun here when I was little?*

I strained to think back as far as I could in my life, but all I could come up with was remains of feelings, flashes of memories like perfume on the air when someone walks by.

Eventually, with a sigh of frustration, I kicked off the bedclothes and sat up.

SNNNNNORE SN.. SN... SNORE.

I couldn't stand to be in the bedroom anymore.

As quietly as I could, I slipped out of bed and, on my bare feet, I tiptoed out of the room and closed the door behind me. To my surprise, I wasn't the only one awake. A light from the living room shone a thin silvery crack under the door. Peeking around the door, I saw Tom lying on the couch, playing an intense game on his Game Kid through squinting eyes. He looked up, stunned for a second, but relaxed when he realized it was me.

"Sleeping here sucks," he whispered.

I nodded and stepped further into the room.

"Believe me," I replied. "It isn't any better out there." I sat down on the end of the sofa and pulled Tom's comforter over my legs. "I don't think we'll be getting much sleep this week."

Tom sighed. "And I really like sleep, too."

We sat and stared at the far wall for a while. The cabin didn't even have a television. What sort of evil place didn't have a television?!

We sat and listened to the creaking sounds of the cabin settling, and the croaking snores of Dad that even the walls couldn't stop.

"Well," Tom said, sitting up. "If we are here, we might as well look at the photo album." He reached under the sofa and pulled out the black covered book with the golden word ' Memories' on the cover. He brushed off a layer of dust and opened the book. It took all I had not to snatch the book from his hands and hold it protectively to my chest. Whatever was in there, they were *my* memories. I wanted to protect them.

As Tom turned to the first photo, I took a slow breath. We both leaned forward and looked at it.

Mom stood on a beach in a colorful dress, the sun setting on the horizon behind her. In both of her hands, she held wooden sticks and the tips of the sticks were on fire! She grinned at the camera.

"Woah," said Tom. "Is that your mom?" I nodded, the words sticking in the back of my throat. "She's really hardcore."

Tom turned to the next page and gasped.

My dad stood on the same beach, dressed in rainbow colored swimming shorts. He was holding the same sticks as Mom, except a third one was spinning through the air above him and he was looking up at it. He was juggling with fire!

"No, that can't be Mr. Stevenson..." Tom mumbled, leaning closer to the photo.

It was easy to understand his confusion. My dad did *not* do things like that. Nowadays, he would rant about safety and the dangers of fire and blah blah. Actually juggling with fire? No. That wasn't him at all. Tom turned the page again.

Dad was leaping off the side of a cliff into turquoise water far below. Nowadays Dad squirmed uncomfortably when I ran down the stairs.

Tom turned again.

Dad and Mom gave a thumbs up to the camera as they hung off the side of a sheer cliff by thin ropes, the ground out of sight below them.

"It's like he is a completely different person," I said with a frown. I turned the page this time.

Dad was underwater in scuba gear swimming amongst beautiful colored coral. It looked like a tropical paradise.

On the next page there was a photo of him inside a metal cage. Around him swam humongous sharks, and yet he looked completely calm, reaching out to the nearest one with his hand.

"Your dad is..." Tom struggled to get the words out. "...cool?"

I laughed. My dad wasn't cool! That was ridiculous.

"He *was* cool," I corrected him. "Now he's...well..." I gestured at myself and the boring body that I inhabited.

Tom nodded and continued to flick through the book. After a moment, he said: "What if it *was* him now?"

I looked up from the book. "What do you mean?"

Tom had *that* face on. By *that* face, I mean the one he uses when he is plotting and scheming. He usually reserves it for when we are gaming and up against a really tough challenge (or if I keep beating him – which happens a lot – and he is trying to think of a way to beat me). He stared at the far, television-less wall, and said, "What if we could make your boring dad of now go back to being the cool dad of then? That could make this holiday epic!"

A slow grin spread across my face as I considered the

possibilities. Not only would it make this painful holiday a lot more exciting, but he might also open up more about Mom. "You know what, Tom? That's a really good idea."

"What's a really good idea?" Sarah stepped into the room, rubbing her eyes.

Tom quickly hid the book behind himself and smiled sweetly.

"We were just talking about... stuff," he said.

Sarah yawned. "Stuff?"

"Yep," I said. "Talking. Doing talky stuff."

Sarah's eyes suddenly opened. "Ahhh," she said. "*That* talk. *The* talk."

A jolt of fear spread through my body. I had forgotten about that. Sarah had asked me a few weeks ago to have *the talk* with Tom about 'adult stuff'. I had agreed (because Dad would have agreed) even though I have never had 'the talk' myself. I heard it included stuff about birds and bees. It sounded really confusing.

I had hoped Sarah had forgotten and somehow, Tom and I had stumbled blindly right into it.

"So you feel... *better* now, Tom?" Sarah asked. "That you know... stuff?"

Tom's eyes widened as he turned to me, realizing what she was talking about.

"Er... yeah," Tom said quickly. "Now that I know about stuff and... things."

Sarah looked at me. "What have you talked about?"

My eyes darted between Sarah and Tom. They both looked at me expectantly. I had no idea what to say.

"We just covered the basics, you know? Important things that he needs to know for life and stuff."

Sarah raised an eyebrow. "Life and stuff?"

"So much life and stuff," Tom nodded in agreement.

There was a pause.

Sarah smiled. "Good," she said with relief. "I'm glad. You mind if I join you on the sofa?"

She sat down next to me after I scooted along.

"My room is *filled* with bugs," she said. "I don't think I'm going to get much sleep tonight."

"Join the club," I said.

Sarah rested her head on my shoulder and smiled. "OK!"

Tom scowled at me from the other end of the sofa.

Why is it never simple?

Down Town

When I woke up, golden sunlight was streaming in through the cabin's windows and Tom's bare foot was pressed firmly against my left cheek. At first I didn't understand what was going on, tiredness clouding my mind. It felt like I was back in the lake, unable to make out anything around me. But then the cheesy smell of his toes entered my nose and I held my breath, gently pushing his leg away while he slept next to me. I tried not to gag.

The morning didn't get any better from there.

A scream from the bathroom woke everyone up, and we all left our rooms to find Sarah running out of the bathroom with a towel wrapped around her head.

"Sarah? What's wrong?" I asked as she ran around behind me and hid.

"A...a...rat!" she said. "In the bathroom! A furry evil little beast! And it's so *filthy* in there, David! Oooh, I need to sit down."

Tom guided her to the kitchen while I peeked my head around the bathroom door. Because the bathroom light didn't work none of us had used it the night before. No one was brave enough to go in there in the dark. Luckily, there was a separate toilet. But the first thing I noticed when I entered was that the room smelled *worse* that Tom's feet (I didn't think that was possible) and everything seemed to be covered in a brown layer of grime.

"Eww..." I whispered. Then I saw it. A brown flash of fur dashed across the floor towards me, almost as if it was out for my blood! I couldn't help but scream myself, and slammed the door closed just in time to hear a soft *thump* on the other side.

Tom looked at me from the kitchen.

"Don't go in there," I said.

Tom shook his head. "I never plan to."

63

So now we couldn't sleep *or* go to the bathroom on this holiday. It was getting better by the second.

But the worst thing about the morning? It was Dad.

Dad was totally oblivious to everything. He was happy, he was relaxed, and most of all he kept saying, "Ahhh, what a *great* night's sleep I had," to everyone.

As we all gathered around the remains of Greg's pie for breakfast (we didn't have any other food left), Sarah broke the silence.

"I think we should head down to town today. There's a bus every half an hour and the thought of staying in this cabin *one second longer* is driving me insane."

Tom and I nodded in agreement. We also wanted to be as far away from the cabin as possible.

Dad frowned. "What's wrong with the cabin?"

Usually, when I think of vacations I think of sun, sand, relaxation, more ice cream than one human could possibly eat, swimming in the sea, stuff like that. For a brief moment, I pictured in my mind my dream island holiday destination.

But that image was quickly wiped away. So far, I had nearly drowned, had slept on a sofa, had seen a rat and generally was about as relaxed as a man sitting in an electric chair.

A math exam would be better than this, I thought to myself glumly as the small bus chugged its way around the small, winding roads towards the nearby town. Trees fluttered by outside as we tried to get comfortable on the strangely lumpy chairs. None of us talked. I stared out the window and tried to list the good things so far about the cabin. I hadn't even thought of one when my eyelids began to droop with the gentle rocking of the bus...

"Hey!" Dad shook me awake. "We're here."

I sat up. "Ergle bleh?" I mumbled, wiping a line of drool from my mouth. Following Dad off the bus, I squinted in the sunlight, blinking a few times. I had stepped into a completely different world.

The lake here was bustling with activity. People were on rowboats fishing, some people swam in the water, others sat on large, expensive boats drinking sparkling glasses of champagne to show off how fancy they were. And that was *just* the lake. The town behind me was filled with shops and people all walking and chatting, enjoying the sun. Suddenly, I felt like I was on holiday.

I grinned. "Yes," I said. "This is more like it."

Tom tugged on my sleeve. "Woah, look at *that!*"

Cutting through the water like a knife, a silver speedboat whizzed across the lake faster than I had thought possible. Four people in the back of the boat screamed with enjoyment, holding up their hands and laughing. It looked like great fun! "Wow," I said. "That looks really exciting!"

Dad nodded. "Ah, you saw it too. I'll admit, it is quite a thrill."

I turned to Dad, shocked that *he* would want to go on the speedboat. Was Fun Dad coming back already?

No. No, he wasn't.

He wasn't even *looking* at the boats. I followed his

gaze and couldn't help but grimace when I realized what he was staring at. Of course, the one place my dad would want to go to, even on a holiday.

The museum.

It had a big sign out front that read:

EDUCATION IS FUN!

I shuddered. *Nothing* could make me want to go in there.

"Oh, a museum," Sarah said. "You really want to do that, Jack?"

Dad turned to her. "Education is *fun*, Sarah, can't you see the sign?"

I had to resist the urge to strangle him right there. *EDUCATION IS NOT FUN!* I screamed at him in my mind. An idea popped into my head.

I laughed, loudly.

"Oh Jack, you joker," I patted him on the head for emphasis. "You don't have to pretend you want to go to a museum just to make your old dad happy!"

Dad turned. "But..." he began.

"No, no, no," I waggled a finger at him. "This is *your* holiday as well. I insist we do something *you* want to do. Like... oh, I don't know..." I pretended to look around the lake. "Hmm. Oh, I know, that speed boat! That looks like a lot of fun, doesn't it, Tom?"

"So much fun," agreed Tom.

Even Sarah smiled. "Yeah, that does look pretty awesome."

"I... but..." Dad looked back at the museum as if his favorite puppy had just been taken away. He sighed. "Yes, I suppose I would want to do that."

Tom whooped and began to run towards the docks.

"Yes, but *how* safe is it?" Dad asked for the hundredth

66

time as he checked the clippings on his life jacket.

"So safe, dude," the long-haired guy driving the boat grinned. "I only had one person fall out once and we were going so fast it was like *splat,* you know? They only broke, like, two of their arms."

Dad frowned. I could tell he was about to say something only a boring teacher would say, so I interrupted him. "That won't happen to you, Jack. Just chill."

"Yeah," the long-haired driver nodded. "Chill, dude. This guy gets it." The driver held out a fist and I fist bumped it.

Sarah laughed and shook her head. "You're a strange one, David Stevenson."

"I'm one of a kind," I grinned back.

Tom scowled at me again.

"The worst kind," I added quickly. "Just... so bad."

Sarah was about to reply when the driver kicked the boat into gear. It ROARED into life like an angry lion. "LET'S DO THIS!" he shouted.

"No, no, no, no, no!" Dad clenched the side of the boat and screwed his eyes closed.

WHOOOOOOOSH!

I was pinned back on my seat as the boat shot forward and a wild grin spread across my face. I could hear Sarah behind me doing a combination of a scream and a laugh. Tom cheered and threw his hands up in the air.

Water sprayed up from either side of the boat, splashing us as the driver turned a sharp corner to avoid a couple on a rowboat. We shot out into the open waters of the lake and I heard a deep roar of laughter burst out of my throat as adrenaline kicked in.

We twisted and turned and Dad continued to cover his eyes. He was missing out!

I held onto his arm and pulled it down then he stared, wide eyed at the boat.

"Arrrrrrgh!" he let out a piercing scream, his face

white as a sheet.

Suddenly, the boat came to a stop. The driver turned around.

"Did someone get hurt?" he said. "I heard a woman screaming!"

We all looked at Dad, who folded his arms and stood up. "I want to leave this boat!" he snapped. "It is unsafe and I don't think it appropriate for a child of my age."

The driver's face twisted as his brain tried to figure out the words that had just been spoken.

"Dude," he said. "You sound like a teacher."

"I don't care," Dad said, sticking his nose up in the air. "This is not fun. Not at all. I want to leave."

Sarah stood up too. "Come on Jack, it isn't *that* bad," she said.

"Nope," he said. "I disagree. Get me off this boat now."

I stood up too. Dad wasn't being Fun Dad. If anything, he was being even *less* fun than usual. I felt defeated.

"Fine," I said, sadly. "You can get off the boat right now."

"Thank you," Dad sighed. Then he frowned. "Wait-" SPLOOSH!

Dad didn't have time to react as I shoved him into the lake!

Tom burst out laughing. "Classic!" he said.

Dad spluttered and coughed, trying to stay afloat in the lake. "I'm going to drown!" he shouted. "Help me!"

I leaned over the edge of the boat. "Believe me," I whispered. "You aren't." I poked his life jacket and he stopped flailing. "Also, don't you know how to swim?"

"Oh," he said. "Yeah."

"David," a stern voice came from behind me. "That wasn't very nice."

I flushed with embarrassment and turned to face

Sarah. "Sarah, I..."

SPLOOSH!

Cold water wrapped around me as I ended up in the lake *again*. Sarah had pushed me in!

As I emerged on the surface, she was crying with laughter up on the speedboat.

After I spat the water out of my mouth, I started laughing, too.

Greg and Stacy's Cabin

When we returned to the cabin, each laden with a heavy bag filled with provisions, we found a note stuck on the door. Putting my bag down on the floor, I pulled it off and read. It said:

Howdy!
    I hope you're all having a great time. Come round to mine and Stacy's cabin later tonight and we'll properly welcome you with a feast!
    See you later!
    Greg.

Sarah read it over my shoulder and let out a little squeak of excitement. "Oh, maybe I can use their *shower!*" She clapped her hands together.

The rest of us turned to look at her.

"What?" she mumbled. "I like to be clean..."

We left for their cabin about half an hour later. As we rounded the corner into the grove where Greg's cabin was, we all stopped. I let out a little gasp. What stood in the clearing among the trees was not just any old cabin. It was a wooden *palace.*

Standing three stories high, this wooden gem made our cabin look like a worn-out cardboard box. I was convinced one of the rooms inside could have actually contained the whole of our cabin *and* the car *and* there would still be room to dance a tango.

Tom poked me in the side, "Why doesn't *your* cabin look like that?" He shook his head and gave me a smug grin.

Sarah poked him. "Don't be rude."

"Yeah," I said. "Don't be rude, Tom."

70

Tom stuck his tongue out at me. I stuck my tongue out back at him.

Standing in the center of the front porch, by a large, intricately carved front door, was Greg, waving at us with a large grin. As we got closer, I leaned over to Sarah and whispered: "Do you think Greg is secretly a king in some country we don't know about?"

Sarah giggled. "It certainly looks like it. I bet his shower is *amazing*."

"David and family!" Greg shouted happily. "I'm so glad you could make it!" He turned back towards his cabin and bellowed: "Stacy, they're here!" Turning to face us, he extended his arms. It was time.

On the walk over, Dad had reluctantly given me some pointers on how to cope with Greg's hugs (he still was trying not to talk to me because of the speedboat incident). I was up for the first hug. I tried not to cringe or flinch, I just extended my arms and took in a large breath. Greg's vice-like arms wrapped around me and he pulled me in. I hugged him back. This time it only hurt a little bit. Finally, after a few seconds, he released me and I took a long, deep breath.

I looked up at his front door and tried to smile, despite every bone in my body cringing at once. A wildly grinning woman appeared at the door of the cabin, her blond hair tied back into a braid on the back of her head. I did a double take. She looked almost exactly like Greg, only without the square glasses. She opened her really muscly arms and took me in for another embrace. I wasn't prepared for how strong she was.

Something crunched inside my body. I was sure of it.

"Welcome!" she said. "It's been years, David! I'm so glad you have come round."

I wheezed a response and she waved me into the cabin.

It wasn't hard to find out where the food was. I just

followed the mouthwatering smell in the air, into a dining room. The table in the center was covered in food that would have been enough for ten people, never mind the six of us. I sat down on the nearest chair and felt my eyes slowly grow bigger than my stomach. Everything looked amazing and I wanted to put it all in my mouth.

When we were all sitting around their dining table, I noticed how large the dining room was. It felt like it was somehow *even bigger* on the inside of the cabin. Every inch of available space on the wall was filled with family pictures of Greg, Stacy, and what I assumed were their children, although they were close to Dad's age by now.

"We built the whole cabin ourselves," Greg said proudly, resting his hand on Stacy's.

I nodded along while piling food onto my plate. I noticed that, even though Sarah was talking to them, she was doing a similar thing. She glanced up at me and grinned. I grinned back, taking a bite out of the nearest slice of cheese on my plate.

"It was the first year we were staying in this place that we met David and Lana," Stacy said.

A hush fell across the room.

I stopped chewing on the cheese and glanced up at Dad.

Lana. It was Mom's name. Dad's face was as red as if he were choking. He took a long sip of his drink.

Greg glanced at Stacy like she had broken some unspeakable promise. No one seemed willing to say anything, and with each passing second it grew more uncomfortable. Dad stared into his plate and didn't move. Sarah avoided eye contact with everyone.

I decided to break the silence. "Yeah," I said. "That was a looooong time ago. Aren't we all so old now?"

There was an almost audible sigh of relief from the room and Greg broke out into a grin.

"Sure was, buddy," he said. "Oh, that reminds me!"

He stood up and scurried out of the room like a giant beaver. Everyone left at the table glanced at each other uncomfortably until he finally came back holding a bottle of a brown liquid. He handed it to me and I looked at the label. It was old and faded, and clearly hadn't been used in a while.

"Stone Island Whisky," I said. Uh oh. Alcohol.

Dad's eyes widened as I said it and he dropped something onto his plate loudly. *How am I going to get out of this one?* I thought to myself.

"The very same," Greg said. "Remember it?"

I shook my head. "Nope." I offered the bottle back to him, silently praying that that would be the end of it.

Greg almost looked disappointed, but then he pulled out a glass from a nearby cupboard and poured some of the liquid into it. "Perhaps this will jog your memory."

"I don't think that-" I began

He handed the glass to me. I glanced at Dad who was shaking his head, his eyes open wide. He *really* didn't want me to drink this.

Oh well. I thought. *How bad could it be?*

"Bottoms up!" I smiled, raising the glass to him and flicked back the liquid.

For a moment, nothing happened. It tasted like I imagined licking the green stuff off the bathtub back at our cabin would.

"I don't see-" I began, then I stopped as my throat burst into flames! The heat spread all over my face and down into my stomach and I had to grip onto the table so I wouldn't try to pull my face off. "ARRRRRRRGH!" I shouted. "WATER!" I choked. "WATERRR!" I groped around on the table, until my hands wrapped around the jug of water and I began to chug it like there was no tomorrow. Greg and Stacy laughed.

"Ahh, yes," Greg said. "Whisky was always Lana's favorite drink more than yours."

The cool liquid calmed the fire in my throat, but I could still feel it warm inside me.

"But enough about the past. Who is *this* beautiful woman?" Greg smiled at Sarah, who blushed in response.

"You're too kind," she said through a mouthful of bread.

I was still coughing and choking when Stacy asked: "How did you two meet?"

Tom rolled his eyes.

Sarah grinned and looked at me. "Tell them the story, David. I'd like to hear your version of it."

"Er..." What was *the story* that she was referring to? I had no idea. I searched my memory for anything that could be considered a story that my dad liked to tell. All I could think of was how obsessed he was with telling me to clean my room. How *did* my dad and Sarah meet? I mean, I was hanging out with Tom a lot, but I didn't really know the details. "Oh well, Sarah and I... er..." I fumbled to find something to say. "Sarah's great," I smiled awkwardly. "You tell it Sarah, I'll let you."

Sarah frowned. "It's better when you tell it, David."

"I don't think so," I said back.

"Never mind then," Sarah said, eating some more.

The uncomfortable silence fell over us again.

Dad closed his eyes and sighed.

"Right," Greg said quietly. "OK."

Sarah looked at me and I could tell she was hurt by what I had said. I silently kicked myself. I was meant to be *dating* her and all I could say was 'Sarah's great'? What was *wrong* with me?

Sarah stood up. "Do you need help washing up?" she said to Stacy.

"No, dear, of course not," Stacy said.

"Please," Sarah said. "I insist." She glanced at me as she carried the plates out of the room.

I'd messed up again.

The Dream

The next day Sarah was distant. Every question I asked she answered with a single word or less. She regularly found excuses not to be in the same room as me. Sometimes she would whisper something to Tom, he would sigh, walk over to me and ask me a question that she had clearly wanted to ask me, but wasn't happy enough to acknowledge my presence. I had really messed up. I had to figure some way to sort it out and fast.

For the most part, Tom was loving it. He clearly loved the distance between me and his mom, and he didn't even try to hide it. He bounced around, happy as a bumblebee in spring, and focused on trying to get 'cool, fun Dad' back. On the second morning, he placed a list of things to do down in front of me and Dad, and said: "I have the *rest of the vacation* planned out!"

Dad and I glanced at each other and looked down at the sheet of paper.

TOM'S AWESOME LIST OF HOW TO MAKE THIS VACATION THE MOST AWESOME:
1. *SKY DIVING*
2. *SCUBA DIVING IN THE LAKE*
3. *SKY DIVING INTO THE LAKE WHILE WEARING SCUBA DIVING EQUIPMENT*
4. *MOUNTAIN CLIMBING*
5. *SKY DIVING OFF A MOUNTAIN*
6. *SKY DIVING OFF A MOUNTAIN INTO THE LAKE? (WILL CHECK MAP)*
7. *SPA DAY.*

I looked up from the list, confused. "Spa Day?" I asked.

Tom shrugged. "I like massages. I'll check on my

phone to see how close the nearest airfield is!" Then he bounced out of the room.

Dad picked up the list. "Sky diving? Is he serious?"

I nodded. "Deadly, I'm afraid."

It was on the third day that Dad took me to one side and said, "Jack, we *really* need to do something about this thing with Sarah. I think I heard her *crying* in her room last night. She was really hurt by what you said at Greg's cabin."

I felt like I had just taken a punch to the gut. Crying? I didn't realize it was *that* bad.

"What should I do?" I asked him.

"Well, you could...er..." Dad scratched his head. "Well..." He tapped his fingers against his lips and clicked his tongue. "I guess..."

Finally, he sighed. Neither of us had any idea what to do. It was a complete disaster.

We were in town later that day when Sarah walked off on her own because she needed 'time to think'. Now, I have enough experience with girls to know that when they need 'time to think,' you are in deep trouble. Something had to be done. I pulled out my phone and glanced at the signal. Luckily I had a few bars, so I called the only person in the world who knew something about girls and making them feel better.

I called my girlfriend Holly.

I mean, I'm pretty sure she's my girlfriend. Maybe. Kind of. It's complicated.

I felt my hands growing sweaty as the sound of the phone ringing echoed in my ear. What was I going to say? The last contact I had really had with Holly was watching her hug Dad after the school fair. She had seemed happy at that point. I didn't want to risk messing everything up with her as well.

But I didn't hang up in time.

"Hello?" The sound of her voice in my ear made something tingle in my heart. Or maybe it was the strange hot dog I had eaten earlier from a street vendor.

"Er... Hi," I said.

"Jack?" she replied. "Is that you? You sound really weird."

Right. I thought to myself. *I have Dad's voice.*

I quickly came up with an excuse. "Yeah, sorry, I have a throat infection. Really bad. Makes me sound like a gorilla. Also, the signal is bad. "

"I'm sorry," Holly said. "That sucks."

"You have no idea," I agreed.

"What's up?" she asked.

I took a breath. How was I going to explain this to Holly without giving everything away? I mean, the last time I had tried to confess everything to her, she ran away and thought that Dad was going insane. I'm still not one hundred percent certain I *haven't* gone insane. Although I tried pinching myself and it hurts, so at least I know it isn't a dream.

"I have a ... friend," I began. "He needs help."

"Uh huh," she said. I could almost hear her eyes narrowing on the other end of the line. "How?"

"Well, I...er... he has a girlfriend but she is not happy with him at the moment. He messed up big time."

"I see."

It occurred to me then that she might think I was talking about her and me.

But I wasn't.

Was I?

Girls are so complicated.

"He needs to make things right, but he doesn't know what to do. He said some stupid things, which he regrets."

"Well, an apology would be a great place to start," Holly said.

Of course! Why didn't I think of that?

"To start?" I said.

"Yeah. She also needs him to make her feel *special.*

You can apologize to anyone, but for her, he should go further. Make her feel wanted."

I frowned. How was I going to do *that*? "Uh huh... wanted."

"I think your friend can figure it out from there." she said. "If the relationship is destined to last, it will all work out."

"Destined to last... right," I said, trying not to think about what it would mean if we *weren't* destined to last. "Got it. Thanks Holly, you've been a big help."

"I'm amazing." Holly agreed. "Keep in touch more, yeah?"

"OK," I said. "I will. Bye, Holly."

"Bye, Jack."

Make her feel *wanted*. I assumed she didn't mean 'Wanted: Dead or Alive'. Or did she?

No, of course not.

I still had no idea what to do.

That night I lay in bed and stared at the ceiling again. Not because of Dad's snoring - I had cleverly bought some earplugs in town - but because I was still trying to work out what I needed to do in my head.

I tossed and I turned and I tossed and I turned. But eventually, I drifted off into a light sleep.

"Hey, Jack."

Even though I hadn't heard it for years, the voice was instantly recognizable to me. I sat up in bed and realized I was back at home, silver moonlight shining through my bedroom window. Sitting on the end of my bed was Mom, looking exactly as she did the last time I had seen her, when she took me to school. She smiled warmly.

"Mom?" I asked. She leaned forward and hugged me. Even her smell was the same, a flowery, warm kind of smell that reminded me of home. She began to pull away, but I didn't want to

let her go. Tears rolled down my cheeks and I hugged her tighter. "I didn't think I'd ever see you again."

She laughed. "I'm always around, Jack, you know that." For a while she was content to just let me hold her. She rubbed my back with her hand and hummed softly.

"Everything's so hard," I sniffed. "I'm trapped in Dad's body and being an adult is hard and... and..."

"Shhh, I know," Mom kissed my cheek. "But remember, it isn't easy for your dad either."

I frowned. "What do you mean?"

Mom pulled back slightly. "Did you ever stop to think why he isn't 'fun dad' anymore?"

I opened my mouth and closed it again.

She nodded. "He doesn't do crazy things anymore because of you. You're the reason."

"Me?" I asked.

"He wants to keep you safe, Jack. You're the most important thing to him."

I was so busy thinking about me this whole time, I didn't realize that Dad was thinking about me as well. Realization hit me like a train and tears were streaming down my cheeks all over again.

"I've been so stupid," I groaned.

"No, never," Mom said. "I'm proud of you, Jack, you're doing really well. I just need to you to do one thing for me."

"Anything," I said.

"Make your dad think about himself more, think about Sarah more. He needs to stop dwelling on the past, to stop thinking about me and how good it was. You need to show him what he has now. Can you do that?"

"That sounds difficult," I said. "How will I know what to do?"

She looked at me, her blue eyes filled with love. "You're a smart boy. You'll figure it out."

"OK, Mom. I promise."
"I love you, Jack." she said.
"I love you too, Mom."
She smiled.

My eyes opened. I was awake, my face pressed firmly into my pillow. As I pulled away, I realized it was wet with tears. I smiled a little. Something that I thought had been missing from my heart for so long suddenly seemed to be there again.

Not only that, but the solution to the Sarah problem suddenly appeared in my mind. I knew exactly what to do.

I poked Dad until he woke up.

"Urgh?" he said.

I grinned. "Come on, Dad," I said. "We have a lot to do today."

Fixing the Sarah Problem

The first part of the plan involved getting Sarah and Tom out of the house. I'll admit, I might have gone a *little* too far.

Tom was still asleep when I came back inside after heading out to get what I needed. The morning air had been cool and fresh when I walked around to the generator, a glass jar in my hand. I had moved quickly because it was *super gross* and I didn't want to think too hard about it. When I opened the living room door as quietly as possible, I saw that Tom was sprawled out on the sofa again, GameKid in one hand. I crept over to him, whispered: "Sorry, Tom, it's for the greater good," and emptied the jar of little red spiders all over him.

I felt bad doing it.

I felt *terrible* doing it. I mean, this was my *best friend*.

Then I sneaked out of the room and back into my bedroom.

Dad shook his head. "You're *sure* they aren't dangerous spiders?" he asked.

I nodded. "Positive. I checked on the internet like fifty times when we went to town the first time. They don't even bite."

"AAAARRRRRRRGGGGHHHHHH!!!!!"

The scream echoed all over the cabin.

"He doesn't know that, though," I said with a grin.

Sarah rushed to the door and was about to open it when Tom burst out, running around in circles. "Spiders!" he shouted. "Spiders all over me!"

They were all over his face and arms. It made me shiver just to think about it, but then I got into character.

"Oh no! Tom, let me help you!" I picked up my towel

81

and began to hit the spiders off him. Sarah joined in too. We managed to get most of them off.

"How did that happen?" Sarah asked.

"I... I don't know!" Tom said. "I was just sleeping and they were crawling all over me when I woke up!"

"Did any of them bite you?" I said.

"What?" asked Tom.

I grabbed him by the shoulders. "Did any of them bite you, Tom? I have a cream if they did, and you need to apply it soon or you'll get a *horrible* rash."

"A rash?" Tom's eyes widened.

"A *horrible* rash. Itchy boils which leak pus. Really gross. Luckily I had the cream last time and applied before it got bad." I nodded knowingly.

"What kind of spiders were they?" Sarah said.

"A bad kind. Not too poisonous, but annoying. I think the scientific name is the *Itchysupernastyaria spider.*"

"Oh dear," Sarah said.

Dad called to me as he rushed into the room. "Dad! Bad news!"

"What is it, son?" I asked.

"We've run out of that cream you were using!"

"What?" I said, my eyes opening wide. "Oh no! You'll have to go down town to get some!" I said to Tom and Sarah. "Maybe even to a doctor, pronto!"

"Pronto," Dad added, as if that would help at all.

Sarah frowned and, for a second, I thought it wasn't going to work, but Tom stood up and began to gather his clothes. "I don't want a rash!" he said. "I need to get to a doctor!"

"Pronto," I said again. I *like* that word.

Sarah grabbed the car keys. "Alright, we'll go down to the town and see if we can find a doctor. You are both OK up here by yourselves?"

"Perfect!" I said.

"Pronto... I mean, great!" Dad said.

Sarah took Tom in her arm. "Come on, Tommy, let's sort you out."

And like that, they were gone. We were alone in the cabin.

Fixing the Sarah Problem – Part 2

As we watched the car drive away, Dad sniffed and said: "How long do you think we have before they figure out the spider... What was it called?"

"The *Itchysupernastyaria spider*," I grinned.

"Yeah, *that*, doesn't exist?"

I shrugged. "Long enough, I hope." Now we just had to put into motion the *second* part of the plan. We went back inside the cabin, pressed our ears gently against the bathroom door and listened. For a while, all I could hear was the quiet sound of us breathing. Then:

Scuttle scuttle scuttle.

"Maybe it's just a tap dripping?" Dad asked hopefully.

Scuttle, scuttle.

"Maybe?" I replied, even though I was completely sure it was the sound of tiny feet scampering around the wooden floor of the bathroom.

Scuttle, crunch, crunch, scuttle.

"How do you think we can get it out of there?" I asked.

"I've been thinking about that and..." Dad walked into the nearby kitchen and came back out with a bucket. "Ta daaa!" he said. "The latest in rat catching technology."

I looked at it. "A bucket?"

Dad nodded.

"To catch a rat."

"It will be simple, right?" Dad grinned.

Wrong. He was so wrong.

Less than a minute later, I was crouched down by the edge of the door with the bucket in my hands.

"Why do *I* have to catch it?" I asked.

"Because you are the responsible adult," Dad said with a serious face.

I growled at him. "I think you are enjoying this too much."

Dad put his hand on the door handle and gave me a thumbs up. "So much!" he grinned. "Ready?"

I took a deep breath. "Alright let's..."

Dad didn't wait for me to finish. He opened the door and revealed the small bathroom to the world.

The gross stink drifted out of the room. I wiggled my nose and held my breath.

We waited. Everything was silent.

It was still silent.

"Maybe-" I began.

scuttle Scuttle SCUTTLE!

A small brown flash zoomed towards me! I slammed the bucket on the ground with a triumphant roar. We had caught it!

"I got it!" I yelled. "I can't believe that worked!"

"Er... Jack..." Dad said.

"I mean, a *bucket*? It seems a bit crazy if you think about it."

"Jaaaaack..."

"But here we are, with a rat in a bucket."

"Jack, it's not in the bucket," Dad said with a panicked voice.

"What do you mean?" I said, suddenly very aware of a warm, heavy feeling on my back.

"Don't move," Dad whispered.

Slowly I turned my head. A brown face with a long twitchy nose and two black beady eyes stared back at me from my shoulder.

Rats, it turns out, are a *lot* scarier and bigger in real life than you would think they are.

I kept completely calm and focused on the plan. I just needed to get the rat into the bucket.

"ARGH!" I screamed, jumping up, feeling the little rodent dig its claws into my back. I spun around and around and the rat squeaked in shock trying to hang on, its pink tail flying through the air behind me.

"Stop Jack, stop!" Dad shouted, but I wasn't listening. I ran to the open front door and leaped out onto the ground outside, colliding hard with the muddy floor. The rat, finally releasing my back, flew off into the nearest bushes with a triumphant squeak. It paused to look back at me, as if to say *I win*, and then disappeared.

I lay on the ground, panting, trying to stop my throat from closing up in terror. Dad, being as helpful as ever, stood in the doorway and laughed.

"Well, that way works too!" he said, spinning the bucket on his finger.

"Yeah," I said. "Great."

I spent the next few hours on my hands and knees, with a peg on my nose, scrubbing brush in the other hand, trying to get rid of the thick layer of grime that had built up all over the bathroom. After about half an hour, I stopped thinking about what the grime could be and just got to work. *It's for Sarah,* I told myself. *Just do it for Sarah.*

I didn't throw up, but it was very, *very* close sometimes.

Meanwhile, Greg, with the help of Dad, replaced some of the moldy wooden beams outside the front of the cabin with brand new ones. When I told him it was a present for Sarah, Greg was more than happy to help out. Stacy even joined in: she brought us a cake with Sarah's name spelled across the top in strawberries.

When the car finally pulled up again outside the cabin at the end of the day, it almost looked like an entirely different place.

Sarah, confused, was directed to the clean and fresh smelling bathroom, where she was allowed to finally have the shower she had been waiting for all week.

Then, once she was clean, we all sat down for a meal in the kitchen, the cake with her name on it in the middle of the table. Before we began to eat, I stood up, holding a glass of water in front of me. "To Sarah," I said. "I'm sorry I got caught up in the holiday and forgot what was *really* important which is, of course, you. You're great," I grinned. They were the *right* words this time.

Everyone cheered, even Tom, who later admitted that Sarah was really upset all day and it was a relief not to have her complain about me anymore.

Sarah stood up, smiling, threw her arms around my neck, kissing me on the cheek. "You are terrible, you know that?" she said.

I nodded. "You choose to hang out with me. What does that say about *you*?"

"You're walking a fine line, Mister," she said and hugged me again.

I think the plan might have just worked.
I glanced at Dad. He was smiling too.

Into the River

When I woke up the next day, Dad seemed a completely different person. I was drawn to the kitchen, following a smell of bacon which made my mouth water, and found him already awake and preparing breakfast for everyone. As I entered the room, he grinned at me, placing bacon and eggs onto a plate in front of Sarah, who eyed it hungrily.

"Hello!" he said cheerfully, turning back to the next serving that was still sizzling on the frying pan behind him. I sat down next to Sarah and a plate was placed in front of me as well. She only paused for a second from chewing on her mouthful of food to say:

"I didn't realize you enjoyed cooking so much, Jack!" she said. "This tastes amazing!"

Dad walked over to me, patting me on the back as I forked a salty cube of bacon into my mouth. "I was inspired by my dad and his *amazing* cooking skills."

The bacon lodged itself in my throat and I choked on it. Dad smacked me hard on the back, dislodging it straight away. "I am an inspiration to all!" I said, once I could finally breathe again, but then wondered if I was complimenting *myself* or Dad. Dad didn't give me time to think about it.

"So great," he agreed.

"Mmm," Sarah said sarcastically. "You look very inspirational with ketchup around your mouth."

I grinned, spreading more ketchup around my mouth like it was a gross lipstick, and then I blew a kiss at Sarah.

"Eww," she grimaced and we all laughed.

When Tom finally arose from his sleep and joined us in the kitchen, the rest of the morning was spent joking and having fun. It was like a weight had been lifted, and we were finally starting to relax into the whole situation. Dad even suggested, once we had all finished, that we go for a walk in the nearby mountains and see what we could find. Tom, who believed this was a sign that we were the closest ever to finding 'Fun Dad,' agreed with the idea with such enthusiasm that he nearly pushed us all out the door.

The journey to the mountain was longer than expected, but it didn't do anything to dampen our spirits. We all joked and sang along to songs on the radio in terrible voices. As she drove, Sarah kept looking at me and smiling. It was a relief to know that I had fixed the problem. She was now behaving in a completely different way to the previous few days and had even offered to drive. I couldn't help but smile back. This vacation was finally starting to feel like a vacation.

When we reached the mountain, the sun was high in the sky and the weather was hot. The trees around us were a lush green that you only find when you are far from cities, and the air smelled fresh and clean. We all put on backpacks filled with snacks and drinks, ready for the walk ahead, and set off along a dusty path through the forest, the mountain rising up ahead of us.

As we walked among the trees, the only sounds to be heard were the singing of the birds, the whoosh of the wind through the trees, and Tom laughing loudly as he messed around with Dad. They raced each other up the hills, hid behind rocks and trees, and constantly challenged each other to bigger and bigger tasks. *Maybe we have found Fun Dad,* I thought to myself as I watched them. *Maybe it has all worked out.*

"This is great," Sarah said suddenly, breaking my train of thought. "I'm glad we are all here."

I nodded. "Yeah, it did turn out alright, didn't it?" A little smile broke out on my face. For the first time in weeks, I felt relaxed. I thought back to home and to Holly. Maybe I could bring *her* here some time. *Would Dad allow it?* I watched him run past me again.

"Yeah, I feel like we are..." Sarah paused as Tom ran

past us. I looked at her and saw that her cheeks had flushed red. When she next spoke, it was quiet, almost like the meaning of the words would run away if she spoke them too loudly. "... a family."

I didn't respond straight away. I just watched Tom and Dad hanging out, how we all seemed to fit together as a unit, all playing our own role, but willing to let the others in as well. I smiled. "Yeah, I suppose so."

Sarah smiled at me and pushed on forward, chasing after Tom when he got too close.

As the path continued to wind its way through the trees, we found ourselves following a river, the sound of running water in the distance slowly getting louder and louder. It almost sounded like it was raining in a torrent when we turned the next corner, but we quickly found out why.

"Awesome!" Tom said.

The clearing was something out of a fantasy novel. A waterfall tumbled off high rocks into a small lake. It then branched out through the trees towards the path we had been walking along.

"Last one there's a rotten egg!" Dad shouted, charging past him.

"Hey!" Tom said. "No fair!" They set off in a race towards the waterfall and Sarah moved close to me again. I could feel the warmth of her body near my left arm.

"David," she said.

"Yes?" I turned and found her staring at me intensely. She leaned towards me. Alarm bells went off in my head. *DANGER DANGER! KISS ALERT!! KISS ALERT!* She was trying to kiss me! Instinctively, I took a step back and slipped up on a rock. Sarah grabbed out for me, only to fall as well.

SPLOOSH!

The water from the stream began to seep into my pants. It was c...c...cold.

Sarah, lying on top of me, burst out laughing. "Oh David, only *you* could do that!" She tried to roll off me, but managed to get our backpack straps tangled, causing her to fall closer to me. Suddenly, her face was very close to mine, her brown eyes taking up most of my vision.

"This water is very cold!" I squeaked.

The tip of Sarah's nose poked mine.

"Hey!" I heard Tom's voice from nearby, angry, breathless. "Get off my mom!"

He charged down the bank of the river as Sarah managed to undo the straps of our bags and helped me up. As I got to my feet, Tom positioned himself between us, forcing me to take a step backwards, further into the river. I felt my shoes fill with stream water.

"Leave her alone!" Tom said, his face twisted. "You promised!"

Sarah tried to calm him down. She knelt in front of him. "Calm down, Tom. It's OK, we just fell into the stream."

"He was trying to *kiss* you, I *saw* it!" Tom snapped.

"I wasn't!" I began. "Honest! We just fell over."

Dad was standing on the bank now, watching the scene with a concerned face. I began to walk towards dry land again, but Tom stood in front of me and scowled.

"Listen, Tom," Dad said. "I think..."

"I don't care!" shouted Tom, not even turning to look at him. He placed a hand on my chest and shoved me backwards a step. "Stay away from my mom!"

Sarah stood up now, her face furious. "Tom!" she shouted. "That's enough! You have gone too far!"

"But, Mom..." Tom said, turning to her.

"No," she said. "David can kiss me and I can kiss him if I want to! You aren't in charge here, Thomas!"

Tom mumbled and fumbled, his face flushing red. "But he *can't* kiss you," Tom said, my secret on the tip of his tongue. "Because..." I flinched. I could already feel my world crashing down around me.

"Enough!" said Sarah. "I know you want to control this, but you *can't.*" she said.

"But you *can't* be with him," Tom said quietly.

"I can be with him, Tom," she said softly. "I'm in love with him."

"You're *what?*" Dad said, his eyes widening.

"You *what?*" Tom shouted.

The water was flowing freely through my shoes and socks now, but I couldn't feel it. *Oh no,* I thought. *This is bad.*

Back at the cabin

The best way to describe the journey home would be a word that I have just made up right now. That word is: *SuperreallyOMGawkwardnotawesomeatallwowhowdidwegethere.*

It's a pretty long word, but I think it describes with great accuracy everything that was rushing through my mind as everyone tried desperately not to make eye contact with each other.

Just don't ask me to spell it, OK?

To really put the icing on the cake, as we drove back along the winding roads, where we had laughed and joked on the way towards the mountain, we now sat in silence and watched dark, angry clouds roll over the landscape ahead of us. As we got closer to the cabin, the same clouds began to spit out lightning and rain.

As the car came to a stop, Tom got out and stormed off towards the cabin, slamming the door angrily behind him.

"Tom!" Sarah shouted, chasing after him.

I sat with Dad in the car and we listened to the sound of the rain rattling against the metallic roof. I closed my eyes and sighed. How had we got *here*? Everything had been completely fine this morning.

"Well," Dad said after a moment's silence. "That could have gone better."

I nodded, staring at Sarah who was trying to calm Tom down underneath the porch. Tom looked back at the car, shook his head and disappeared inside. Sarah followed him.

"*You* know I wasn't trying to kiss her, right?" I said, looking anxiously in Dad's direction.

Dad smiled at me. "Don't worry, son, I believe you."

I breathed a sigh of relief.

"She was definitely trying to kiss *you* though," he said

with a smirk. "Perhaps you should stop pretending to be me so *well*."

I turned towards him. Somehow, in a strange way, he was *enjoying* this.

"She keeps trying to do that. I don't know how to avoid it, but at the same time I don't want to do anything stupid to ruin it," I groaned. "It's like trying to juggle chainsaws."

Dad chuckled at that. "Welcome to adulthood, Jack. It's non-stop excitement. Let's get inside."

As he opened the door, cold air rushed into the car. Even though the distance was nothing, it was raining so hard now that we were completely drenched by the time we reached the cabin. Thunder crashed as we closed the door behind us, and Dad reached for the light switch. *Click.*

Nothing happened.

Click click click. He pushed it a few more times, just to be sure. There was no denying it. The power was out.

"Great," Dad mumbled.

BOOM.

Thunder shook the windows of the cabin.

Sarah's scream echoed from the living room.

We charged inside and found her standing by the far wall, rubbing her head sheepishly.

"Is everything alright?" I said.

Sarah grimaced. "Sorry, the thunder made me jump. I head butted this cupboard." She pointed at the cupboard at the side of the room.

"Is the cupboard OK?" I asked.

A small smile played on Sarah's face, even though she tried to stop it.

"What's that?" Dad said, pointing at a piece of paper on the floor.

"It fell off when Mom hit it," Tom said quietly from the sofa. He had his phone raised up in front of his face. It was his way of trying to ignore everyone when he was grumpy, but I knew he would be watching me and his mom closely.

Dad knelt down and picked up the piece of paper, blowing off a layer of dust that had accumulated over it. I realized that the paper must have been on top of the cupboard for years. I leaned over to see what it was.

Uh oh.

It was an old hand-made card. It had been made years ago, from blue paper. On the front was a rainbow, scribbled onto it in crayon with the words 'Happy Father's Day' written under it in a black pen. It looked like something that would be made in a kindergarten project. Slowly, Dad opened the card and looked inside.

I tensed up. It was another relic of the time long passed, of a time when Dad and Mom were together and we were a family unit. The last thing I needed at this moment was Dad storming off again, I thought to myself, but there was nothing I could do.

What actually happened, however, was completely different. Dad smiled and began to chuckle, and then slowly, it grew and grew until he was laughing his head off!

For a second, I thought Dad had completely lost it.

He stood in the center of the living room and he laughed and he cried, and his whole body shook as he did so. Everyone looked at him in confusion.

"Are you OK?" I asked him.

Dad finally began to calm down. He handed me the card, still chuckling, and I looked inside.

This is what it said:

To Daddy,

After every storm there is a rainbow. I'm sorry I broke your laptop. Also
HAPPY FATHER'S DAY!
Love from Mommy and Jack

Mom had written my name neatly alongside hers. I don't think I was even old enough to hold a pencil when this card was made.

Dad looked out the window. "After every storm, there is a rainbow. Lana's favorite quote," he said quietly and then: "*Mom's* favorite quote," a bit louder, for Sarah and Tom. "Seems pretty fitting right now."

We all looked at the dark storm that raged outside. It was getting worse with every passing second. I hugged myself subconsciously.

"What does it mean?" Tom said, standing up.

"It means," Dad said, "that life is crazy. Life can be tough. Sometimes everything goes wrong and it seems like there is no hope." He grinned. "...But you have to *smile*. You have to know in your heart that it will get better. That's how you get through the stormy times."

I smiled a little. I guess Mom was always filled with useful advice for everyone.

Sarah laughed. "That's beautiful." She moved over to Dad and put her hands on his shoulder. "Your mom was a real smart lady."

"She was," Dad nodded.

Squeak.

The sound made us all turn in unison towards the doorway. The rat had somehow made its way back in!

"Ugh!" Sarah said, leaping away from the door.

It was Tom's turn to burst out laughing. He stood up on the sofa where the rat couldn't reach him and laughed out loud. "That's *horrible*," he choked.

I laughed too. I couldn't help it, it was contagious.

"The storm," Tom laughed. "No electricity, a rat in the house...." he wiped a tear from his eye. "It's the worst!"

"The whole vacation has been awful!" I agreed through body-shaking belly laughs.

Soon everyone was laughing. It was like all the frustration and the stress of the last few days was being forced out of our bodies. The rat looked at us like we had all gone insane. Maybe we had.

Dad grabbed Sarah by the hand. "This way!"

"What?" she said. "No, I..."

But Dad wouldn't let up. He pulled her out the door, passing the rat, who watched with interest, and then right outside! He danced around with her in the rain and they laughed as they spun around in circles.

I glanced at Tom. He shrugged. "I guess it's too late to say no?"

"That's right," I grinned and soon we were dancing outside in the cold rain with them. We laughed and we danced, the water washing away the pain from earlier. As Dad, Sarah and Tom formed a conga line to go around the cabin, I stopped for a second and, through the rain, I thought I could see a figure standing on the porch. She leaned on the wall and watched us all with a smile.

Mom. I thought to myself. *We did it.*

Another crack of lightning shook the world around us, and we danced like it was a hot summer's day.

Going Home

On the final night of the holiday, I slept like a log. When I woke up, Dad had already packed all of his clothes and was halfway through packing mine. He glanced at me as I sat up in bed and yawned loudly and shook his head. "Next time we come here," he said. "Try to pack *more* than four t-shirts. I think I smell like old cheese," he sniffed his armpit and grimaced.

"No change to usual then," I joked.

Dad threw a t-shirt at me as I laughed. I narrowly avoided it but it was true, it did leave a smell of old cheese in the air.

By the time I was up and dressed, the cabin was looking more and more bare. I was surprised by how much we had managed to fill it up in the short time we had been here.

"Leaving today then?" Greg stood in the doorway, holding a pie in his hands, as I dragged my suitcase from the bedroom.

I nodded. "I'm afraid so."

"Stacy made you another pie," he smiled sadly. "I hope you enjoyed your stay."

I awkwardly accepted the pie from him and balanced it on the end of my suitcase. The plastic plate it sat on was still warm.

"Always," I grinned. "We'll try to come more often from now on. We'll see you next year?"

Greg's grin grew wider at that. "Absolutely, buddy. I can't wait."

"Well I..." Greg moved forward and crushed me with a hug before I could finish what I was saying.

When he finally released me, I tried not to cry out as my bones returned to their normal positions.

"I'll miss you," he said. His eyes got a little misty.

"I've... gotta go..." he stumbled out of the house.

What a weird guy.

Sarah was already standing by the car when I reached it. Even though we had plenty of room in the trunk, she was still trying to find the optimal place to put each bag so that it would take up the least amount of room. A small pile of suitcases, neatly stacked, took up one side. There was still enough room for a fully grown adult and a bike on the other side.

"Do you need any help?" I asked.

Sarah smiled, forcing her bag into the trunk with a final push and turning to pick up mine.

"No, I'm good," she smiled. "I think Tom might need a hand packing inside though."

"Alright," I nodded walking away.

"David?"

I turned back to her. She lifted her hand up to her lips and blew a kiss at me.

I grinned and caught it in midair.

When I knew she had turned back to the car, I wiped the kiss on my top. I didn't need any more trouble right now.

I found Tom dragging his bag down the steps in front of the cabin. He stopped as I reached him and looked at me with narrowed eyes.

"Jack," he said quietly. "I know you're my friend and have been for years." He leaned in closer. "But if you don't find a way to swap your body back with your dad soon, I swear I am going to tell her everything."

I was speechless. He didn't wait for an answer; he just took his bag and carried on towards the car. I felt a shudder go through my body. He was serious. Deadly serious. For the first time, I looked at Tom in a way I never thought I would. I *didn't trust him anymore.*

It didn't feel good.

Dad came out of the cabin shortly after.

"I think we are almost ready to go," he said. "It's been

100

a bit of a crazy vacation, eh?"

I nodded, pushing down my feelings about Tom into a small box inside me. I would think about them later. "Crazy. Not very relaxing, now that I think about it."

Dad laughed. "Yeah, I don't think Dr. Turner is going to like that."

We both stared at the cabin fondly, letting the fresh air and the smell of the forest fill our lungs one last time.

An electronic piano started playing.

"Oh, that's my voicemail," he said. "I'll just get that."

I continued to stare at the cabin as Dad walked away. "Bye, Mom," I whispered quietly, a warmth filling my heart. "I'll see you next year."

I turned towards the car, but paused when I saw a deep frown on Dad's face as he listened to his voicemail. He raised his hand to his mouth as if he had just heard something horrifying and looked up at me with something in his eyes that I didn't like: fear. He listened a bit more, then walked over to me as he hung up the phone.

"What's the problem?" I asked, the peace from earlier dripping away, replaced by a cold, nervous feeling in my gut.

"It's.... it's about my job," he said. He took a deep breath. "Something about the fact that Dr. Turner got in touch with the school. Mr. Thomas has found out and is lobbying the governors of the school against me."

I blinked. There were a lot of words there that I didn't understand. But I could just imagine Mr. Thomas causing trouble in any way that he could.

"But what does that all mean?" I asked, frowning as I stood there waiting for him to explain.

"You coming?" Sarah's voice cut across the field. I turned and grinned, but it felt like a mask.

Dad put his phone back into his pocket and turned towards Sarah with a smile. "We'll be there in a second." He turned away again and took a breath. "I'm going to be fired,

Jack. I won't be allowed to teach anymore."

As soon as he had spoken those words, he took a deep breath and erased the look of fear from his eyes, replacing it with a smile. He ran towards the car like any child would do and shouted: "I want to sit in the front."

"Too late!" Tom shouted back and they play fought to try and get in the front seat.

I was left behind, and as I slowly walked towards the car, I tried to consider the implications of what he had just said. What would happen if he lost his job? How would we be able to keep living where we were?

"Are you alright?" Sarah asked as I got closer. "You look like you've seen a ghost."

I smiled at her, and lied again. "It's nothing. I'm fine.

Let's go home."

But one dark thought kept hovering in my head as I closed the car door behind me. *What will be waiting for us when we get back?*

***

Find out what happens next in
Body Swap
Book 4
Available Soon!!

Thanks so much for reading my book.
If you could leave a review, that would be awesome!!
I can't wait to hear what you think!
Katrina ☺

Remember to subscribe to our website
Best Selling Books For Kids

You can select any single ebook of your choice for FREE!

We will also keep you updated on all our new releases,
special deals and send you further free books from time to
time, just to say thank you for being a valued subscriber.

Like us on Facebook
And follow us on Instagram
@juliajonesdiary
@bestsellingbooksforkids

Here's some more funny books that you're sure to enjoy…

And here's some more great books...

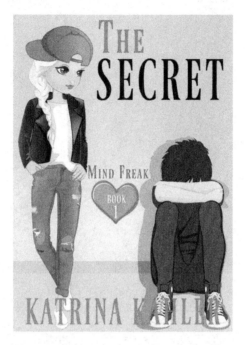

CPSIA information can be obtained
at www.ICGtesting.com
Printed in the USA
FSOW03n1953191016
26359FS